Tales From Between: One

A Strange Literary Journal

Ai Jiang, Matthew Stott, Ivy Grimes, Gemma Amor, Patrick Barb, Nikki R. Leigh, Christi Nogle

TALES
FROM
BETWEEN

Contents

Between You and Me

Why start a new literary journal? It's madness. Do you just enjoy throwing your money out the window? Because you won't make a profit, you know, even if you try to keep costs low. You're going to lose money on every single issue.

Hello and welcome to *Tales From Between*. Each issue of this journal will feature a gathering of the fantastical and the horrific. Dank, improbable stories from a range of different authors, from the up-and-coming, to the established, to the never-heard-of-them.
We like stories. We hope you do, too.

On you go then, *Strangers*, read well...
Matthew Stott

Please consider supporting us on Patreon and help us continue to publish strange stories!

patreon.com/TalesFromBetween

FOLLOW US ON TWITTER: @from_between

Naked Shark

by Christi Nogle

The Seafood Shoppe was a bad idea from the start. The three of them were getting passive aggressive about the food even before then. No one asked for what they wanted but instead argued for the food they insisted the others wanted, and so they would often compromise or land in terrible little places—smiling, saying, "Well this looks nice" even though the places were thoroughly wretched and cursed and everyone knew it.

But the Seafood Shoppe was busy, and that's always a good sign, isn't it? Busy when they came through on the way to their Airbnb, busier when they went souvenir shopping, busier still when they stopped after a day of aimless beach-wandering. The Seafood Shoppe beckoned with fluorescent signage and kitschy shit all around—swags of buoys and plastic crabs and painted wooden fish stuck in old, frayed netting. Picnic tables in yellow and pink and garbage cans overflowing with paper plates and shells, seagulls and yellowjackets swarming around.

And maybe Lou, her husband Carl, and her sister Bea were feeling too disheveled to go someplace nice. Maybe that was part of the reason they stopped here. Carl looked just about as he always did, but Lou's face was shiny and her blouse all wrinkled with a spot of ketchup still visible from a spill at breakfast. Bea had a line of sunburn at the top of her forehead carrying up into the part of her hair. God, even little sister Bea's hair was going gray now, if you looked closely. And so maybe they didn't feel they deserved someplace nice.

Once they'd parked, they got a better sense of the general age, fitness, cleanness, and . . . wellness of the clientele. Though Carl and Bea made a point of not looking at each other unless it was absolutely necessary, there were shared looks between Lou and Carl as well as between Lou and Bea. *What the hell is wrong with these people?* said those looks. They wouldn't have dreamed of saying anything out loud (well, maybe in the car later), but they noticed. Oh sure they did. Not often do you see a crowd of forty or fifty people with more than just a handful of missing limbs or with so many bruises, bandages, and angry-looking stitches. At least two obvious colostomies, besides.

"This will be good, I think," said Lou as they got in the long line snaking out the door. She was too hungry, or "hangry" as Carl said, to think of going anywhere else.

"Authentic, anyway," said Bea. The breeze stopped, and the smell grew stronger. Fish and frying oil, crab meat, sauces, and garbage like you would expect, but something else, something like piss. Was it from the woman just ahead of them? She had a dark stain on the crack of her pants; Bea couldn't say for sure that it was pee but rather hoped it was.

"We can still do the Pancake Palace again. They have salads," said Carl, massaging Lou's shoulders because he knew she was getting *hangry* now. He was so tall he had to stoop down to rest his chin on the top of her head, which he often did. Lou still liked the big goof mauling her in public. Bea was, frankly, embarrassed by their displays of affection. Even here.

As they approached the door, Bea could read some of the signboard prices (not cheap) and smell the ammonia growing stronger.

"It's the shark smells that way," said a gorgeous low drawl behind Bea. She turned and saw a friendly-looking man her age with a large, dark bruise on his jaw and some bottom teeth missing. All his other parts, though. Handsomest man at Seafood Shoppe.

"Oh yeah?" she said absently.

"Most places marinade it out, but here you get it . . . naked," he said eagerly.

She nodded and turned away.

"You going to get some?" he said to her back.

"I'll stick with crab cakes, I think," she said.

It didn't seem like he was going to respond, but slowly, quietly, the sound built. "*buk-buk-buk- buk-buk-BUK-buk-buk*." He was calling her chicken!

Bea only scoffed.

"What are you, a *tourist*?"

And though she was, obviously, a tourist, this pissed her off so bad that when their turn finally came, she pushed past Lou and Carl and not only ordered naked shark for the table; she also paid.

Lou and Carl, cheerful from their cuddling, made that gesture above their heads: minds blown.

———

Carl went up when their number got called and returned with three thick steaks resembling rose quartz, each with two dark bruises (veins?) above a gaping fault. With unwashed fingers, Bea turned the frown on her steak into a grin.

"No fries?" said Lou.

"I guess they don't come with. I'll—"

"No way," she said, pulling Carl down. "Let's just eat."

They did, with an unusual lack of bickering—no talking at all, really. Bea locked eyes with Mr. Handsome across the way as she took her first large forkful.

There was an objectionable flavor, but none of them focused on the flavor. As soon as they began eating, a strange feeling came over all three of them, a feeling that none of them knew they were sharing with the others. Adrenaline, panic, excitement like you feel chasing something or being chased. Each bite brought greater and greater urgency, and yet they were calm enough on the outside.

They ate quickly, and soon they were wiping juices from their lips with napkins that already seemed slightly used. They massed their garbage on the tray and sent Carl to dump it. Lou and Bea, sitting on the same side of the yellow picnic table, watched his sinuous movement, tracked him across the yard. They focused on the long dark line of sweat down the back of his t-shirt.

He lifted the lid on a can too full to add one more thing, put the lid back on, turned the tray upside down on top of it, and gave a goofy chuckle.

"Yeah!" a big man nearby said. "Yeah, show 'em, those pigs."

Mr. Handsome, too, hooted his approval.

Carl pumped his fist in the air and waved the women to follow. It was time to head back to their Airbnb.

The urgent feeling didn't leave them. Bea drove, and Carl and Lou shared the backseat. Her fingers ran up and down the slickness of his spine under his T-shirt. They were all hyper-alert, jumpy, not speaking but sometimes making little murmurs of enthusiasm and warning. Pedestrians staggered too close to the road, and the cars on the opposite side often looked to be coming straight at them. Bea kept pressing the brakes and accelerating again. When the tailgaters honked, Carl and Lou swung on them, teeth fully exposed, middle fingers thrusting.

The urgent, avid feeling kept up as they entered their "cottage." Bea beelined for the bathroom, as was her privilege. She stayed on the little sofa in the sitting room while Lou and Carl had their own cramped room for sanctuary, so they let her run over them in every other way.

The two of them tiptoed back to this room now, thinking to make a little "flippy-floppy" as Carl called it, but the air was nauseatingly hot and stale. When Carl bent over to take the stick out of the sliding-glass door track, Lou pinched his ass hard. He swung around to grab her and she jumped out of reach. *Open the door,* she thought. *I'll chase you.* He didn't read her mind, not quite. He read the jutting gesture of her chin. She was slick with sweat and had lost her blouse somewhere. Her baby blue bra was drenched see-through. The belly she never exposed to any light looked firmed, plumped, and blindingly bright above dark yoga pants.

They both felt as keyed up as they had back at Seafood Shoppe, but each had the idea they were acting normal. Neither suspected the other of feeling what they did or of having any clue what magic was happening inside them.

Out they went, Carl and then Lou a moment after, for a long run around the village of gray-shingled cottages, circling out into the neighborhoods and then the long hills leading to the beach. Carl ran fast, gave her quite the chase.

Bea stepped out of the bathroom and back in to check the toilet had flushed. The cottage smelled overwhelmingly of pee.

With a moan, she stripped off her little sundress. She stepped through their open bedroom door and threw the dress atop a pile of clothes. *I feel peculiar*, she thought, tossing herself face-down on their bed. Mr. Handsome sprang to mind. Bea imagined she was back at the yellow table, eyes locked with his. She imagined hurtling toward his table, teeth exposed, belly-hovering through the air toward him. It was a strangely arousing fantasy. To savor the replays of it, she rolled over onto her back and held her arms and feet close to her body. She swayed to the right and to the left in the bed imagining hurtling through the air toward him, taking him—and then taking them all—all of the Seafood Shoppe customers. One by one and two or three at a time, sinking her teeth into necks and legs and stumps, butting them away with her powerful head, lashing them with a powerful tail. They screamed but they loved it. She shuddered. A breeze came through the door just then, bringing up goosebumps.

Bea still wore her thick black bra but had lost her Spanx shorts somewhere, so that when she groped her way out onto the little porch, a woman on the opposite porch called "What you doing, Ma'am?" The woman had two little kids she was tucking back through her own sliding-glass door.

Bea exposed her gapped teeth and hissed air through them.

"Hey," called a man getting groceries out of the back of his SUV. "You can't—"

Just then a naked man rushed past, knocking the grocery sack out of his arms. The man ran on for about fifty feet and stopped short, turning. Mostly hairless and entirely naked. Not Mr. Handsome but just about comparable. Friendly face and a friendly gesture that seemed to say, *C'mon, honey. Chase me. What are you waiting for? Don't mind these tourists.*

He turned and ran in the direction of the pink-and-blue sunset, and from the distant beach came a cheer like you hear in the summer in town when the fair and baseball games are going on.

Excited, aroused, Bea shivered. She shoved her feet into the nearest sneakers, which were not her own, and ran bottomless past the spilled groceries and the gaping tourists in the cottage village. She ran along the streets of the neighborhoods, up and down the long hills leading to the beach. The hairless man slowed when he sensed her coming, and when she was close enough, he sped up to give her a good chase.

The cheering grew louder and morphed into screams. Beach grass prickled under Bea's feet and then the running got harder in strength-sapping sand. She crested the last hill and stopped short.

The man was bent over panting, his balls hanging comically low. The beach lay before him, vast, stunning, and full of life—full of battle. Chases were ending in mouths full of blood, sleek powerful tackles, joyous cries and screams.

Bea felt someone behind her. She swung around to find Mr. Handsome himself, nude but for the sweaty, sagging bandages around his ribs. He gave a gesture that seemed to say, *Go on, then. Only fair we chase you a while, ain't it?*

Bea bared her teeth to him and turned back toward the beach. On her mark, set. She was no chicken. Maybe she was still a tourist, but after tonight? No, after tonight she'd be one of the crew.

AUTHOR BIO

Christi Nogle is the author of the novel *Beulah* (Cemetery Gates Media, 2022) and the forthcoming collections *The Best of Our Past, the Worst of Our Future*, *Promise*, and *One Eye Opened in That Other Place* (Flame Tree Press, 2023). Her short stories have appeared in over fifty publications including *PseudoPod, Escape Pod*, and *Dark Matter Magazine*. Follow her at http://christinogle.com and on Twitter @christinogle

Lakeside Ceremonials

by Patrick Barb

(Content Warning: childbirth, extreme violence)

Betty knew no one came to Camp Arbor during the winter. Snow blanketed paths snaking between trees. Cabins stood like plague houses, boarded-up and forsaken. The camp and surrounding town of Arbor's Mill couldn't handle outsiders once ice and snow settled over the area.

Even though she'd long ago abandoned her "Counselor" t-shirt to the cleaning rag pile, Betty personified the "Camp Arbor" way. And after thirty years of living nearby, watching the campgrounds, she'd found, if not peace then, an order of sorts.

All to have it thrown into jeopardy by the unaccounted-for arrival of *the girls*.

It's not fair, them coming here. Not now.

The girls' presence in Arbor's Mill, the questions they'd asked about accessing the campgrounds off-season, their youth, and beauty, all those factors combined to set in motion *His* return. Pressure to move up her normal timeline manifested like a vice around Betty's head. Her ears popped with every step taken across the ice-covered lake at the center of the campgrounds.

I shouldn't be here. They shouldn't have come yet. It's too early.

Given their slow, unsteady progress to the frozen lake's center, Betty had time to consider all of the things she'd rather be doing—snuggling up under a checkered-pattern blanket with Keith, lying by the fireplace at his bed-and-breakfast, letting him do the *thing* with his thumb pressing against her inner thigh.

Keith was a good listener.

Instead of chaste marshmallow-flavored firelight kisses and the touch of curly salt-and-pepper beard hairs against her neck, Betty contended with teeth-grinding pain ping-ponging through her aching, freezing muscles. Her atrophying joints crackled like campfire kindling at even the slightest bend.

The heavy duffel bag she'd taken from the trunk of the nosy deputy's patrol car, filled with road flares and sundry items for poor souls lost in the cold, caused her to stoop forward. She walked with a hunch, like some tired old maid. *It's how I feel.*

But she couldn't stop. Stopping meant throwing away thirty years of sacrifices, and she'd worked too hard, given up too much, to let it happen.

It's such a shame we're here when the lake's so miserable.

Betty wished the girls waited until the days got longer and the sun's rays shredded the icy covering. In the summer, algae and sunscreen scents wafted off the water's surface even when the camp was inactive. Out in the cold, her snot stuck fast between her nostrils and upper lip. She inhaled the copper-sweet scent of the deputy's blood diffused in the chill night air.

The way the back of his head and everything inside misted the snow. Got him right before he made it to his radio too. Then, those girls understood I wasn't leading them out here for whatever "film project" they wanted to make.

Betty held Keith's shotgun in the crook of her right elbow. Its padded butt pressed against her descending breast. She aimed its long, lewd barrel at the backs of those girls, all bundled up tight in thick winter coats and Etsy scarves, hair tucked under woolen caps. Those layers hid the decadence of skin, sin, and sex for two of them and the unspoiled innocence of the other.

But how to explain the swell of the good girl's belly, visible even under cold-weather clothes, stretching the long white dress so she looks like half a snowman?

"Move," she said, speaking as much to her troubled thoughts as to the outsider trio in front of her.

Inside, Betty chastised herself for questioning the process. She reasoned *He* must sense something more in the girl from his vantage point at bottom of the lake, peering up through the opaque lens of thick-sheeted ice.

Sleeping in the embrace of still waters, *He* waited for them. Betty would bring them to *Him*. It was their arrangement, as far as she understood it.

"Please, don't do this, Ms. Betty. Shawna's not okay."

Shawna. The pregnant girl.

Words came like machine-gun bullets through chattering teeth. "Th-th-think muh-muh-muh-my wa-wa-water b-b-broke... f-f-f-f-fuck!"

I'd never speak in such filthy terms. I was a good girl. No drinking, no drugs, no sex. It's why He chose me.

So, why choose her?

Shawna learned some difficult truths about herself, her body, and the process of bringing life into the world over the nine months since the doctors implanted the fertilized egg into her womb. She learned she was far too agreeable, going along with whatever her best friends Raylene and Zee suggested because she knew they loved her almost as much as they loved each other. She also learned she'd need new shoes when the baby growing inside of her got the boot at last.

Shawna wondered if she'd missed out on the "fun" part, foregoing sex and going right to being knocked up.

Agreeing to surrogate for Raylene and Zee seemed like a good idea. If not a good idea, then the right thing to do at least. She knew her friends would make wonderful moms, but they needed some time to get their lives together. That's where Shawna came in. She offered them a nine-month reprieve.

But as the day approached, the couple and their surrogate learned another lesson: having a baby was expensive as hell.

"Almost 10,000 dollars," Zee said, "But we have a..."

"...plan." Raylene finished.

It was the tag-team approach they used, each one completing the other's sentences.

"We could sell custom videos. There's a whole mess of perverts online, desperate for salacious..."

"...content. Think what they'd pay for videos, pictures, voice recordings of a pregnant *virgin*. But don't..."

"...worry. We wouldn't make you do anything sexual. We'll film it somewhere exciting too. Like, did you ever hear about..."

"Camp Horror?"

Out on the ice, Shawna learned a new lesson. *Everyone dies.*

And it didn't make her feel special at all.

––––––

February winds slashed and howled, making it hard for Betty to concentrate or even think. She worried those distractions might cost her. After all, she had her secret rituals to perform—rituals keeping her in *His* favor.

In the summer, it went easier. Betty let trespassers, thrill-seekers, and those too dumb to know better come to the lake in their own time. And they came. Again and again. Smelling of cherry lip-gloss, bug-spray, and teenage impossibilities. They were his required sacrifices and Betty offered their unworthy bodies to *His* relentless slaughter.

All except the virgins, would-be pretenders to her "Queen of Summer" throne. She kept them for herself. When she dispatched them, a tingling sensation traveled from between her legs, spreading like a crack in a mirror's glass surface.

Is this what sex feels like? Do you feel this...powerful?

The pregnant girl—*Shawna*—had baby-fat cheeks to go with her plump belly. Yet she'd fought the hardest when Betty forced them out of the back of Keith's pick-up truck, making sure they stepped over the dead deputy's body cooling in the pink snow.

She'd broken the girl when she poked the gun barrel against her rosy, wind-bitten cheek and traced a line down, stopping at her stomach.

Betty chuckled to herself as she realized who the girl reminded her of. She was like the Betty of local legend, the last surviving counselor from the Camp Horror Massacre. The sweet, innocent girl who went along with the story they'd told to her about her—the one where she killed the Masked Man, sending the boogeyman to the bottom of the lake. But it was the story they told, not the story she lived.

What if they knew how their story became the bait in our trap...

Time and again, others came to the campgrounds, perhaps subconsciously drawn to the chance to take part in the lakeside ceremonials. Betty—the *real* Betty—was always waiting. And she found the new girls lacking, unworthy of *His* attention.

I'm the only final girl He'll ever need.

Keith almost ruined everything before the three girls shook the snow from their boots or Betty saw their faces and knew—*they're the ones. His next ones.*

During their early morning "cuddle time," a single "God-dangit!" from Betty proved a more jarring line of attack than a slap to the face or kick to the groin for Keith. Cut to the emotional quick, he sat on the edge of the bed, white undershirt stretched tight above his belly, argyle socks rubbing the hardwood, stringy black and gray pubic hairs, matted and tangled with spilled seed, reaching for his belly button.

Betty pressed herself against the headboard and pulled white sheets up to her chin—making her body a ghost.

"I told you...not inside me! I told you!"

"Aww geez, Bett, I kept it outside. But we were rubbing and it..."

If Keith hoped for sympathy, one look at the flushed red cheeks and the throbbing temple of the woman he called his girlfriend during the slow winter months in Arbor's Mill would've made it clear he'd have no such luck.

"I told you, we can't have sex. I'm a virgin. If you want we can do it in the behind..."

When Keith lowered his eyes and shook his head back and forth from side to side, he made Betty feel like a child. Like, *she* didn't understand the ways of the world. "You know it counts as sex these days, right?" He leaned forward, pawing for his grey flannel pants on the floor.

It doesn't count for Him.

Then, the girls pulled into the parking lot behind Keith's bed-and-breakfast, laying on the horn, announcing their presence to the world. From bed, Betty had a clear view out the window and down to the lot. She watched a brown bunny, late for hibernation or up too early, making a break for it, bounding across the snowdrifts. After all the years, she'd learned to read the signs, the heralding of *His* return.

Yes. I understand now.

She made a quick study of the room. Looking for anything sharp. Anything to bind, bludgeon, or bash. During their initial encounter, she'd thought the fact she'd used her surroundings to her advantage was what kept her alive. Years later, she knew better. But she still believed it to be a good trait to possess.

"Bit early for out of towners, huh?" Keith asked, letting the elastic band of his too-tight cotton boxer briefs snap against his waist. The thick black leather belt he wore looped through his pants had snaked its way over to Betty's side of the bed.

She glanced down at the belt, considering how tight she could cinch it. Then, she noticed the pillowcase behind her, damp and clinging with sweat.

They'll do.

She'd felt sorry for Keith after the deed was done. Not because he'd been slow to fight back, his eyes wet with tears, questions half-formed on his blubbering lips. He'd been slow, but he fought back once he realized Betty's mind was more than made up.

No, she'd felt sorry because it didn't need to happen. She wished he'd listened to her. Wished he'd let things proceed as they always did. But he hadn't listened. He'd injected himself into the ritual and, as a result, he died.

She prayed he hadn't ruined everything.

The girls believed Betty ran the B&B. And why shouldn't they? She'd done nothing to dissuade them and none of the locals passed through the bed and breakfast to say different either. Aside from it being the off-season, everyone in Arbor's Hill except Keith had enough sense to keep their distance from Betty. Since they didn't understand how she came through the Camp Horror Massacre *and then stuck around. They'll never understand why I stayed.*

For Him.

But Betty understood the role the townsfolk played. Their blind eyes turned away gave her a chance to prepare the way for *His* return. Sometimes the camp reopened under new management, sometimes kids came to smoke, pop pills, and fuck. There was even one time a group of sick obsessives held a Masked Man-themed festival at the site.

"I can't do this..."

One of the girls—Raylene—turned and took steps away from the group, away from *Him*. The other girl, Zee, reached for her girlfriend. Their pregnant friend slumped down toward the ice with one less set of hands holding her up. Zee's bare bluish hands shone under the moonlight. She grabbed Raylene's coat.

"Babe, don't..."

"Ohhhhhhhhhhh..." Shawna moaned from the ice, hands on her knees. She didn't look like much of a fighter anymore.

Shawna's keening synced up with the pounding of *His* fists under the ice.

There's too much work left. And not enough time.

Zee pulled her coat free. Raylene's eyes filled with fear, confusion. Betty figured she imagined everything could still be okay.

There's always one who believes it.

Betty let the nightmare tableau play out longer, acting as a voyeur, watching soap-opera private moments unfolding. It was another of *His* lessons she'd put into practice for herself. *Let them do the work for you...*

"I can't, Zee. I can't. She's crazy. She's gonna kill us all. But I'm not gonna walk to my death. I won't."

The would-be runner took a few more tiny steps away, headed toward the old dock where canoes sat bumping against moss-covered pillars in warmer weather.

"Ray, please. Don't leave me. Don't leave Shawna...our baby..."

Betty couldn't pick out everything they said and the intensity of their emotion confused her. Not like she'd never heard of two women in love, she'd just never seen it that way. Usually, what she witnessed added up to nothing more than shallow titillation, co-eds tipsy on wine cooler exchanging topless kisses for the entertainment of their grunting male companions.

Raylene the runner made good on her threats. However, her rubber-soled boots against the slick surface of ice made for a wobblier escape attempt than she might've expected. Shawna flopped onto her back, wool cap popping off her head and exposing damp blonde curls. Cheeks wobbled. Nostrils flared. The long white dress she'd worn—a costume for the "movie" or whatever it was those girls wanted to make—appeared soaked through with dark, mucus-y stains. Frost-dappled embroidery held the material tight to swollen thighs.

Her? Really?

"Oh my God, she's gonna make it..."

Zee's whispered disbelief snapped Betty back to reality. "Shoot," she said, a command and a curse in one word.

She hated that she'd let herself get distracted again.

Taking a deep breath, Betty blew out cold air like pot smoke from a joint passed at a campfire. Raylene had already covered more ground in the time passed than Betty expected and she wasn't sure about her accuracy at the ever-increasing distance. Still, she couldn't let the girl go. *He* wouldn't like it. She lined up her shot.

Ice shifted under Raylene's feet. A mini earthquake rumbled through the ice. A black spray of lake water spurted out like a shaken soda can burst open in a freezer. Somehow Raylene managed to keep herself upright.

Her last mistake.

Betty's heart pounded with reverent joy. A sign! *He* was there. *He* bought her more time. She pulled the trigger with confidence.

One step, two...then the girl who'd tried to run fell face-first on the ice. The smack of her nose breaking and chin splitting carried across the dark, so it sounded as though she'd fallen at their feet. Betty's ears rang, so the screams of the other girls sounded like they came from underwater. Like they were already under the ice with *Him*. Betty took a step back, watching the dead or dying girl. She allowed herself a smile.

Then, the back of her boot crossed something wet and sticky. She lost her balance, falling hard on her ass against the ice. Another fissure broke open in the frozen surface and the shotgun slid right for it. Betty scrambled for it. But it was gone.

Black clouds moved over the moon, obscuring what went on out at the lake. Betty's hands slapped against the ice. Then she held them up to her face. Blood caked the wool of her mittens. The other girls were gone...

She pulled herself up to her feet, slipping a few times in the blood, piss, and shit. Stamping her foot, cracks rippled through the ice. Those black clouds blew away from the moon and she blinked, taking in the horror-show tableau before her.

Zee pulled Shawna away, but in doing so, she'd brought her closer to...*Him*. "No, no, no..."

Betty ran. She fell. Her teeth sliced through her chapped lips and her ears rang with cathedral bell clangs. She wanted to scream, "Stop! I'm not ready for you." But blood filled her mouth, spilling down her chin.

The Masked Man crawled from the hole made by *His* bloodless fists, knocking aside broken chunks of ice on *His* way to the surface. Zee stripped to an undershirt, stepped in front of him, blocking the path to Shawna. The girl's arms looked like twigs compared to the blocky, golem-like proportions of the Masked Man. "Please, don't. My baby."

Betty slipped again. Her palms slapped the ice. Wet with blood and sick, the wool stuck fast. She pulled and pulled, trying to get herself free. Crimson-soaked threads dangled from her palm, fibers embedding under the skin. But she made it. She didn't try to get up again, opting instead to crawl, hands and knees flailing like she'd forgotten how to move.

She wouldn't stop though. *He'd* come back and she wanted to be there. Closer and closer, so she could reach out from the dark and touch *Him*. Under the ice, waiting in still and silent waters, *His* wounds washed clean, leaving skin smooth and rubbery. Softer than she expected every time. When He picked Zee up and tore her arms from their sockets, a shudder passed through Betty's body.

The Masked Man tossed Zee aside. White hands stained red.

Like my hands.

The killer took plodding steps toward the last girl left.

Last, but no, no, not the final girl.

Wrapped up in her friend's discarded coat and sweater, Shawna didn't look into the Masked Man's covered visage. Like she didn't understand what an honor it was to have *His* attention.

Betty pulled herself up one last time. She knew she had to fight. After all, she was *His* final girl. And it's what the final girls did...they fought back when the end came.

Ice crunched under *His* feet with every step. Black eyes under a cheap Halloween mask focused on Shawna. Her arms were cradled to her chest. A tiny naked form wiggled, kicking under the moonlight. A long, membranous growth dangled from the newborn and ran along Shawna's deflating stomach, disappearing back inside her.

Closer, closer. Finally, *His* shadow stretched across Shawna and the child. Then, the new would-be chosen one raised her eyes from the baby and beheld the Masked Man. But she didn't understand. "It's a girl..."

Betty rose from behind Shawna and put her hands around the girl's head. She wrenched, twisting and pulling where the skull met her neck. Harder, harder. Then, there was a crack, like the Masked Man's cement-block feet tromping on the ice. She collapsed beside the dead girl. Panting, crying, but happy.

She'd kept her place for another year.

I'm still His final...

The corpse-pale fist slammed through the ice, missing Betty's head by inches. She looked up and caught sight of a fire raging in the coals of the Masked Man's undying eyes. She'd never witnessed the look up-close before. It didn't make any sense to her. He always saved it for his sacrifices.

She rolled aside, avoiding a foot intended to shatter her arm. On her feet, she yelled...at *Him*. "What're you doing? They're all dead. I'm the survivor. Now I 'kill' you and we do this again in a year."

But he kept moving toward her. Betty looked around, facing darkness on every side. No answers waited for her in the sky, under the killing moon.

She heard a whimper, a phlegm-filled cough, a haunting cry in the night. Realization settled in, ripping away Betty's teenage dreams. "The baby..."

The Masked Man shoved her down. Betty cracked the back of her skull against the ice. Blood gushed, red mingling with white and blue. He twisted Betty's ears hard. Then, he slammed her face into blackened ice and slush. Her broken teeth sprinkled the ice like fat salt crystals.

Wearing a crimson mask of her own, Betty studied her surroundings through a painful fog. She couldn't feel her lips, but a smile etched across her insides.

I always was good at finding something to fight back with.

She rolled to the side, escaping another attack. Bloody woolen fingers reached for the shivering babe. Betty made a fist around the bruise-colored umbilical cord. The baby screamed, an ear-piercing shriek of defiance. In reply, *His* cry emerged as a guttural, water-logged moan. On *His* knees, the Masked Man clawed his way to Betty. No weapons were needed. He'd pull her apart with inhuman hands.

But Betty was a survivor. She wriggled behind the Masked Man. She wrapped the fleshy cord around his neck. And pulled. Tighter and tighter...

Then, it was the Masked Man's turn to fight. He tried to get free, tried to get away. His shambling giant's steps brought Betty up to her tip-toes. The cord tightened between her palms. The Masked Man's attempts pulled the crying newborn from Shawna's lifeless arms. Betty pulled the cord tighter. Tighter. She willed herself to fall, her ass hitting the ice with a crack. She couldn't tell if it came from the frozen surface or her tailbone.

The Masked Man moved with an uncertain gait, awoken too early from his slumbers. Rusted metal at the tips of his work boots cut through the ice. But he slipped. Black eyes bulged under the mask. A swollen tongue pressed against the cloth covering.

Like a deflated balloon, air whistled out and *He* crumpled. The ice snapped, a huge sheet sticking straight up to the sky. Betty's monstrous attacker slid back under the ice, back into the water. She scrambled back from the spreading dark waters. She looked at the hands that killed the Masked Man.

Except, they didn't kill Him.

The baby's cries grew fainter and fainter. As the Masked Man sunk into impenetrable darkness, the child's cord remained wrapped around his neck.

The cord killed Him. The baby—the baby girl—she's the one.

Betty bit into the cord, cutting through fat and gristle. Biting, pulling, tearing. A heavy hand wrapped around her ankle. *Of course.* Always one final scare. She kicked back, heel connecting with soft, spongy tissue. The Masked Man became an afterthought. *He'd* left her and Betty wanted to move on. She crawled away from the ice and scooped up the naked babe, wrapping her up in the coats.

Under an unflinching lunar gaze, Betty held the child close. She found the duffel bag. Moving to the edge of the lake, she put the baby and coats inside the duffel, creating a makeshift cradle. Then, she fired a flare into the sky, watching its arc over the treetops. Then she lit the remaining ones, setting them in the snow around the baby. There was a good enough chance the townsfolk would notice and come to the child's rescue. None of them were smart enough to grasp the role they played. But they always gave flawless performances. Once *His* work was complete, they'd come for the final girl.

But this isn't His work. It's mine.

Blood droplets froze to her broken face. Betty said a prayer to a God she didn't believe in, pleading for the newborn's survival. She envisioned a time years later. Baby Girl's all grown up, heading to a summer camp like Camp Arbor. Sweet, innocent Baby Girl haunted by a phantom face. A dream memory of the bloody, broken woman who'd killed her family.

Ice crumbled under Betty. She didn't fight, but let herself sink into the lake.

It's not death. It's baptism.

Accepting a new role.

Accepting a new name.

The Ice Queen.

Betty liked how it sounded.

The Ice Queen's blue-black lips moved, making a silent promise to *Her* final girl. She'd be waiting.

AUTHOR BIO

Patrick Barb is an author of weird, dark, and horrifying tales, currently living (and trying not to freeze to death) in Saint Paul, Minnesota. He is the author of the dark urban fantasy novella *Gargantuana's Ghost* (forthcoming from Grey Matter Press, October 2022), the talking animal/cosmic horror novella *The Nut House* (currently serialized in *Cosmic Horror Monthly*), and the collection *Pre-Approved for Haunting* (forthcoming from Turner Publishing, October 2023). In addition, he is an Active Member of the HWA and a Full Member of the SFWA. Follow him at twitter.com/pbarb.

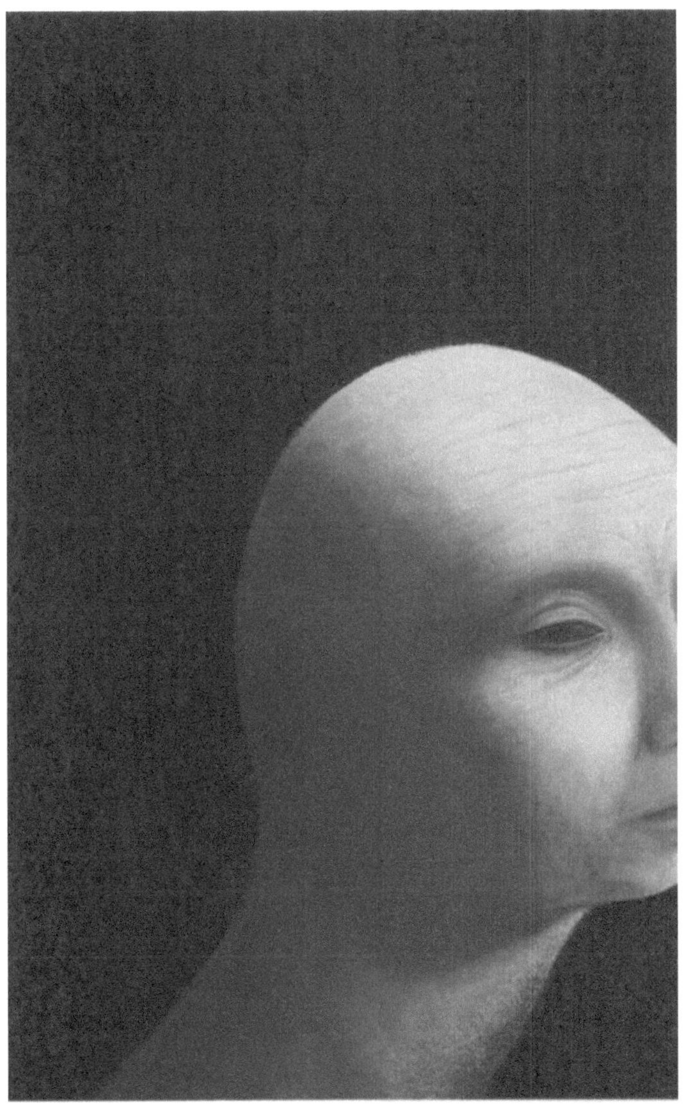

Henry's Legacy

by Ivy Grimes

Nicole worried that Tom was in love with her, so she avoided him as much as possible. She still attended the Anglican church of her youth where Tom was curate, and he had put her in charge of event-planning (which meant making coffee and arranging sugar packets into fans). The congregation hoped Tom and Nicole would get married, but they hadn't even been on a date. Nicole hoped Tom would never ask her out. If he did, she would have to say no since she was already committed to Henry VIII.

Henry VIII died four-and-a-half centuries before she was born, yet she was meant to be his vessel. In her prepubescent youth, the Lord had come to her in nuclear raiment telling her she would bear a son. No virgin birth this time. Rather, through God's transcendent powers, he would transport her to Henry VIII so she could bear him the son he and England craved. She had spent her life waiting for her ticket back in time.

"Why me?" That's what she had asked God. She couldn't remember if that's what the Virgin Mary had asked.

"Don't be so modest," God had said. "You're perfect."

She didn't want to lose her perfection. Otherwise, God would change his mind, and she'd be stuck forever in her time and place giving birth to zero kings of England.

That was why she worked so hard. For example, on the night of the church's Christmas Eve service, she brought enough homemade cranberry bread to feed a hundred members even though she knew only fifty were likely to attend.

Tom arrived early and acted surprised to see her. He contributed to her efforts by locating the paper napkins in her bag and handing them to her. He looked nice in his tweed jacket with his longish hair swept back, but she felt no attraction to him. He was just Tom, an ordinary fixture of a life that would hopefully change as soon as possible.

"What are your plans for Christmas?" he asked, though he must have known.

"My family will have a turkey dinner and sing around the piano."

She concentrated on cutting perfect slices of her cranberry bread and arranging them on a platter.

"I could drop by to sing with you at the piano. I do love to sing."

She looked at him in surprise. He had never been so bold before.

"I'm sure my parents would be happy to see you."

"Your parents will be happy?" His face twitched, hesitating in an incendiary space between horror and hysteria. "Won't you be glad to see me?"

She forced a laugh. "You're our pastor. We're always glad to see you."

She longed to get away from the old routines and still be perfect. She could withstand it as long as she focused on the life to come.

"What's with you, Nicole?" He stood close to her, and she smelled whiskey on his breath. "I'm a man of the Lord and the only Harvard grad you know."

She went over a mental list of all the people she knew. "Cal Thomas went to Harvard. He was a freshman when we were seniors, so you might not remember him."

"He went to Princeton, Nicole, and that's not my point. My point is—do you think you're too good for me? What is it I lack?"

His eyes were a mixture of gold and green, like dragon scales. What did he lack? When she thought of Henry, it was hard to settle in the meantime.

"Love is personal," she began, but she didn't know how to explain.

"What do you know about love?" He gestured with his left hand as if it held a Bible.

"God has another plan."

"God tells me about his plans. I'm his faithful minister."

Tom was so cold and frail compared to Henry. To kiss him would be like kissing a fish.

"You haven't ever heard from God," she said.

"I have, and his plan is for us to marry."

Tom's eyes sparkled with delight or fury. He rubbed his thumb against his fingers and reached out as if to touch her. She stepped away, and he pretended he was only going to scratch his leg.

Their awkward dance was interrupted. The door to the sanctuary creaked open, and Nicole expected to see an early elderly congregant or the choir director. Instead, an all-encompassing brightness filled the room.

"Nicole."

Light like mummy bandages wrapped the newcomer. She could hear him long before she could see him. His voice was much deeper than God's.

"Yes?" She was proud of how calm she sounded.

"It is Henry."

The light faded, but her eyes took time to adjust. She could still see Tom standing beside her, but she also saw the outline of a much grander man walking up to them.

"You aren't supposed to come to me! I'm supposed to go to you. That's what God told me."

"I am here on my own mission," Henry said. Oh, Henry's ruddiness and lightning eyes! It made her want to die. He wore a jaunty black hat instead of a crown, and his broad shoulders were clad in brightest red, like a fresh spring of blood. He said, "It wasn't God who appeared to you. It was one of my trusted advisors who found you as a child and saw you were a handsome girl and a good Anglican. He asked you to wait for me. I've worked so hard, traveling through the years, trying to find a way to save England. My daughter's reign put everything off-track. My legacy was destroyed."

Tears filled his eyes, and the tip of his nose turned red. He lost his manly posture and began to slump.

Nicole had studied English history, especially Tudor history, quite closely, and most historians agreed that Elizabeth was a better monarch than Henry. She had always assumed that Henry must have believed that his—that *their*—son would have been an even better monarch than Elizabeth. He couldn't have been so selfish as to worry about being emasculated by his daughter.

"If you have a male heir, you think it would be better for England and for the world, right? It wouldn't just be better for you?"

He smiled at her, and beams of light escaped his mouth. "My son will represent me in the finest fashion. He'll be the strongest monarch ever to rule. But fate is conspiring against me. I've had hundreds of thousands of male heirs by now with women from every time and place, but nothing works. The boys die young, or they run away, or they disguise themselves so I can't find them."

Finally, Tom spoke. "Nicole, could you call an ambulance?"

She ignored Tom, kept her eyes on Henry. His innumerable infidelities pained her, but she felt firm in her destiny. No other woman had given him what he wanted. She would provide him with his true heir.

He took her hand. "I can see why my advisor thought you'd be a wonderful heir-bearer."

"God has ordained it." She was pleading with him, desperate. He would have to obey God.

"In all my travels, I haven't met God," Henry said. "But I have experienced a timeline with you as my heir-bearer. I have come forward in time to stop the process. It doesn't work, my dear. Our son decides he wants to be an architect, and before he can be crowned, he escapes to the ancient past. I'm so sorry to tell you this. There's so much you can't understand from your vantage point."

"Our son?"

"Yes." Henry put his hand over her heart. "I love you. But the mission is more important than our love."

Her body began to shake as if she'd been electrocuted. Henry's touch gave her both pain and peace. She'd waited so long for it. She and Tom collapsed on the floor, both of them writhing in pain, but she kept her eyes on Henry's beatific face.

Members of the choir discovered Tom and Nicole later that evening. They called the paramedics, but the pair couldn't be revived. In future gossip, the congregation decided that Tom and Nicole were a modern-day Romeo and Juliet, and though some awful twist of fate had kept them apart, at least they had left this world together.

In death, Nicole's soul drifted towards God, but she tried to steer it back to Henry.

AUTHOR BIO

Ivy Grimes also has work appearing in *Vastarien, Dark Matter Magazine, Daily Science Fiction, Shirley Magazine*, and elsewhere. You might find her @IvyGri on Twitter or at www.ivyivyivyivy.com.

A Sea of Grey

by Ai Jiang

The man struggled between two corpses. Although he was used to confined spaces, those were crowded with—mostly—living bodies.

His breath became shallow, but he refused to panic when he spotted the old blood on his jumpsuit.

The compartment reeked, reminding the man of the disposal bins behind the factory at which he worked. There, he often felt like a slab of meat, workers standing elbow to elbow. Sweat and grease of working men and the livestock they handled intermingled. The man left the factory daily smelling of the eight-legged swine he passed along the assembly line. It was indistinguishable as to whether the sweat soaking his uniform was from swine or himself, much like the blood on his jumpsuit.

Within the train compartment, buzzing flies circled his head. He waved his hands in an attempt to swat the flies away but found them immobile—bound like the animals he once slaughtered.

"Hey," a voice whispered.

His eyes flitted towards the sound, but a sea of grey flesh obscured his view. Ironically, it reminded him of his usual train ride to work. It was exactly the same.

His eyes met the dead gaze and ashy flesh of the corpse beside him. He ground his teeth. Although the corpse's dead eyes stared ahead, he couldn't help but imagine that they were looking at him. The dead man's skin resembled the grey jumpsuit he wore—wrinkled and weary.

He shut his eyes, but not before he glimpsed sweat-matted hair and gagged. A shuddering breath escaped his lips, sourness filled his mouth, but it was much better than the pungent stench that would continue to violate his nostrils. He had not yet taken a look at the man to his left and he was not eager to do so anytime soon.

"You alive?"

The man almost laughed. What good would it do to know whether someone else was still alive? His coworkers had asked the same question to a pig after running a knife through its throat. It seemed ridiculous now to imagine his friend staring into the pig's dead eyes with a smile. Sometimes his friend even asked this question to the living pigs. Sometimes, the pigs replied.

After a moment, he decided to entertain his new companion regardless of the absurdity of the question posed.

"Yes, unfortunately," he said. The swine would have offered a similar answer.

A small chuckle.

"Are we lucky or unlucky?" the voice asked a moment later.

The question sounded almost philosophical. The man found himself smiling even given the circumstances.

"Depending on how you look at it," he said.

"Any chance of survival?"

"Perhaps."

A sigh.

The sudden screech as the train braked forced the man and his new companion to stop and listen.

The door of the compartment in front of theirs slid open. There was the sound of the conjoined cows leaving the cart. The weight of the animals, together with heavy steps, jostled the other compartments. Bodies clumsily clashed against one another.

The man stiffened when the faces of the two bodies next to him smacked against his own. The sweaty head of the corpse in front of him collided with his face. Their sweat mixed. He reminded himself not to lick his lips. Just a moment ago, he thought his lips dry, now, he couldn't welcome dryness more.

"I think we're next," the voice said when the door of the compartment ahead of them slid closed, and the train started moving once more.

"I think so too."

————

First it was the ducks—four eyes—because the Michelin restaurants were demanding them for their experimental dishes that quickly overtook all food trends. Then it was the chickens—backless, looked as though they had a thousand arms in the form of wings: a stout, compressed centipede. Chicken wings were already popular in the past, but as they became a staple, a common side rather than fries, they needed not more chickens, but more wings. The man used to work in such restaurants— or at least the man who he is the clone of used to, probably still does. He only had the memories up until the point he was cloned, with his last memory being his original getting scanned at the lab. When he awoke, he was in a cage of sorts, surrounded by the four-eyed ducks, thousand-armed chickens, pigs with fat and muscle too thick and organs impossibly large that shortened their lifespans by two-thirds.

The man was walking through a grocery store with his two children, Lia and Matt—Lia birthed, Matt adopted. A law had passed that allowed the clones to have children, but that could change at any moment—clones were still not seen as fully human. "Animals can breed, so can clones," was the government's rationale. Lia looked nothing like the children of the man's original, and for that she was considered original too, even though her father himself was a clone. But the man often wondered, since he had created new memories of his own, would he not be at least half original? When Lia was twelve, she was quick-witted and at the top of her class. Matthew, though four years older, was far less mature and well-spoken compared to his sister. Matthew was also a clone. His original went to a different school, in a different country. The man was proud of both his children. But the teachers... they never met the man's eyes at parent-teacher interviews, and they were much more excited to talk about Lia than they were when speaking about Matt.

The supermarket aisles were overwhelmed by the number of people covered in grey uniforms, but Lia was thin enough to weave through the crowd effortlessly. The sea of grey some-how never consumed the children. He was always able to keep track of her because of her colourful attire, though there were other adults and children wearing them—the originals. They made a startling minority, yet still... held so much power.

Matthew had a blank stare and grabbed items off shelves or out of freezer sections. The man looked at his son as he trudged behind. The cart in front of him moved not by his will, but was propelled forward by the wave of shoppers surrounding him. He tried to block out the shouting around him and swatted, agitated, at the buzzing hands attempting to swipe things from his cart. Matt didn't notice.

"Dad, can we buy eggs?" Lia pleaded when she suddenly appeared from the sea. "The quadrtiple yoke ones?" At least those were cheaper than the organic, single yoke ones. Her wage once she was older would be able to afford an all-organic diet, the man was sure. He felt the thin wallet in his pocket. Even quadtriple yoke seemed like a luxury now with his fac-tory job.

"Maybe the hextuple yoke one," the man said.

Lia pouted. "But then it's just yoke!"

He patted his daughter's head, and though she continued to pout, she made her way back to the egg section on a new quest.

Lia didn't know about the new laws, the riots they had been causing, or maybe she pretended that she didn't know. Surely, she must have caught word at school. They wanted to get rid of the clones, rid of the biologically engineered animals. For the animals, it was more out of pity, for the clones, it was more out of fear. At least that was what the man believed. There were always too many in their eyes, taking the jobs available, the housing. They, the originals, found the clones disruptive to their lives.

The man looked up at the security cameras scattered across the grocery store, their red eyes honing-in on his sudden movement. When the man finally looked away, the camera shifted to another.

The man and his son somehow made it to the canned foods section. Most of the section was already empty, but Matt grabbed what was left over, batting away reaching ranks extended forth from the rest of the sea around him. Sometimes the man wondered if it was on purpose, that they made it so clones could only afford modified and cloned produce and meats.

Lia appeared once more out of nowhere with four single yoke eggs, cupped in the palms of her hands. He sighed and nodded. The stark white of the eggs stood out against her multi-coloured jumpsuit.

The train stopped again. The chickens stirred from their peace in the compartment behind, a thousand wings flapping, drowning out the sparse clucks. There were periodic dips that bounced the train up and down as transporters moved the chickens out of the compartment. The man didn't have to wonder how many chickens they put in each cage—he and his coworkers were the ones who put them there. There was barely space for the chickens to move, there didn't need to be, and the weight of their wings was far too heavy for much movement anyhow. They'd be disposed of soon, just like the man. The chickens—failed products that didn't meet industry standards; the man—a product that was perhaps far too successful. It had only taken twenty minutes to cram each cage full, but there were more than a few cracks of bones. The man wasn't sure which limb bones severed, maybe it was even the heads, but he didn't want to imagine.

He listened intently, sure his living friend was doing the same.

A screech came from a new voice. "You swine, careful with that."

The man wrinkled his nose at the sound. Well, that answered the question of where the swine went. He laughed to himself.

The train compartment door closed again. The man waited for the train to move, but it didn't. Instead, his compartment door slid open. The man held his breath, but the force of the door opening shifted everything: the cheeks and the matted hair, and the face of the dead man behind the living. Unfortunately, his friend was in the middle of a cough when light shone in.

"Anyone alive?" the new voice squawked.

Silence.

"Good."

Three sudden gunshots.

The man's ears rang and he took a sharp breath. The new voice hummed and closed the compartment door. The train continued on its way.

When the man thought it safe, he checked on his friend.

"Hey," he whispered. "You alive?

A groan.

"Not for much longer..." Then, "By the way, I'm William. Just in case I die."

The man laughed at the introduction. The tragedy of dying without a name seemed to outweigh everything else at that moment for his new friend, William. At work everyone was referred to by their employee numbers. Was there a William? Everything seemed quite absurd now.

"My name is Matthew," he said.

If anyone should be remembered, it should be his son.

"Nice to meet you, Matt."

The man's wife called as he was waiting for his train to work. He stood amongst the other workers who were employed by the same factory. Their uniforms created a unified sea of grey. The man pressed his lips into a thin line.

"Your employer called..."

Then, silence. And after a moment, there was a single unbreaking phone tone. Everyone feared the call because it meant they were no longer necessary. The time would've come sooner or later. The laws, the government, the originals were always against them. They were useful until they rebelled against becoming donors. Some still did offer, living only half a life before they sacrificed themselves for an original. And when that happened, the clones would be praised, but only for a moment, until the anger returned. They'd stopped producing clones now, but there were already far too many of them by that point. The man's supervisors were always making room for new workers—youths dressed in colourful attire like Lia, and looking away from those like Matt, those like the man. One of his friends had been laid off the week before, and another the week before that. Five last month. The man was sure the number would only increase. He had not heard from his friends since.

He placed the phone back into his pocket and squeezed onboard the rush hour train. He had to go to work. There was no choice but to go to work. What else was there to do, anyway? Even if he didn't want to be, he knew he was disposable. They had strength in numbers, but did they have strength in mind? The man thought of his original, the world he enjoyed before the clones, and he felt selfish to try to take that away from the person who he couldn't have otherwise existed without. But were he and his family not deserving as well? Was he in the position to have such thoughts?

He stared at his reflection in the train window. The scenery changed from city to the dark inner walls of an underground passage. His reflection disappeared when the bright daylight shone through the train's windows, and it returned to mock him when the train was again underground. As more people piled onto the train, his reflection became obscured by those who stood between him and the windows, but it didn't matter because they all looked the same. Grey, grey, grey—

Within the compartment, the man couldn't see his reflection when the light of the sun shone in or when the train passed through tunnels. It didn't matter much anyhow. He was unsure if William was still alive and he was too tired to ask. The man also wished to sleep, but he feared that when the train stopped again, he wouldn't be awake.

"Hey, Matthew?" William's voice was barely above a whisper.

The man tilted his head to the side, leaning against the cheek to his left, his energy draining.

"Yeah?"

"Do you have any children? A wife?"

He paused for a moment.

Finally, "No, but I have a mother, Karen and a sister, Lia."

"And your father?"

The man said nothing further, and William didn't ask again because he used his last breath a few seconds later to say goodbye.

The man struggled against the two bodies beside him to see what his friend looked like. Was he the same as the others? Perhaps he looked different. But his efforts proved futile because of the sea of rotting flesh mingling with the colour of soot and ashes all around him.

As the train slowed, he knew it was the last stop. This was always the last stop.

The compartment door opened, and there stood the squawking voice from before. Their face looked as sharp and as bird-like as their high-pitched voice suggested. Flaming red hair sat on top of their head, like feathers. He'd seen him before, weaving through the workers at the factory, pecking at the heels of grey-uniformed men.

"Anyone alive?" they asked.

This time the man didn't hold his breath.

"Yes, I am," he said.

The new voice balked with laugher.

"And you are?" they cooed.

"Matthew."

At the exact moment he spoke his son's name a sharp sound rang through the air.

"Well, Matthew. You won't be for long."

The man gave him the same reply the swine offered his coworkers: the sound of blood gurgling in his throat, loud and defiant, then silence. Before the compartment door closed, he saw the entrance to the factory. He imagined the smoke drifting from the chimneys on top. And within the walls, the smooth assembly line of animals—both alive and dead—passing through the hands stretched out from a sea of grey. Often, it was difficult to tell the animals and the workers apart.

The man turned to his left, knowing, but not wanting to admit, that it was his son beside him all along. His head dropped forward and fell against his son's shoulder. Sweat and blood ran together and it was difficult to tell what belonged to who. But it didn't matter. The last thing he saw was the multicoloured jumper of the supervisor, swirling, swirling, turning grey.

AUTHOR BIO

Ai Jiang is a Chinese-Canadian writer and an immigrant from Fujian. She is a member of HWA, SFWA, and Codex. Her work has appeared or is forthcoming in *F&SF*, *The Dark*, *Uncanny*, *The Puritan*, *Prairie Fire*, *The Masters Review*, and her debut novella *Linghun* (April 2023) is forthcoming with *Dark Matter INK*. Find her on Twitter (@AiJiang_) and online (http://aijiang.ca).

Everything is Fine

by Matthew Stott

'Please, try not to be late home,' said Amy.

Jack Blake couldn't decide what jumper to wear over his shirt. The light blue with the round neck or the dark green with the v-neck. He liked both. The light blue one he'd bought himself, the dark green one had been a present from Amy.

'What's that?' replied Jack.

'Don't be late, we're having guests over, remember?' said Amy from somewhere downstairs.

Dark green. He picked it up out of the drawer and wiggled his head and arms into it.

Jack was almost tall. He had the unruly hair of a nine year old boy and large, vulnerable, hazel eyes.

'You look like a toddler wandering wide-eyed through the world,' Amy had said to him more than once. Sometimes it made her worry about him. Worried that someone might take advantage of him. Other times it was one of the main reasons she loved him.

'How does this look?' asked Jack, finding Amy sitting at the breakfast counter in the kitchen, holding a book in one hand whilst spooning cereal into her mouth with the other.

'Which bit?' she asked, placing the book on the counter. Jack saw it was her almost threadbare copy of *Wuthering Heights*, a book she seemed to read three times a year.

'Sort of, all of it really. Well, mostly the jumper and the shirt. Do they go together?'

Amy smiled and stood, making a grand show of appraising his outfit choice as she walked towards him.

'And this is your choice for a meeting with a potential big, new client?'

'I was going for casual but neat. Don't want to look too try-hard. I think. Or do I? Oh dear.'

Amy wrapped her arms around his neck and looked up into his eyes. 'I think you look awfully handsome, Mr. Blake.'

Jack relaxed. He leaned down and pressed his lips against hers. He had known he would fall in love with Amy Collier on their third date. On their first date he'd been too befuddled by her smile to know if he liked her or not. On their second date they'd gone ice skating and he'd fallen over three times before limping to the sidelines, his rear end throbbing from the repeated sudden impacts. They'd given up skating and retired to a pub, where they'd talked and they'd drank and they'd found everything funny.

And then there was date number three.

'Hi, Jack, you haven't been waiting long in the cold, have you?'

He'd looked at her, enveloped in a warm coat, a long scarf wrapped twice around her neck, her eyes shining, her cheeks glowing, and he'd just known he had to kiss her. So he did.

'I was wondering when we might get around to that,' Amy had said when their lips had parted.

'Was it...okay?'

Amy had smiled, taken his hand, and led him into the cinema, his heart jitterbugging.

'I think you look professional,' said Amy, kissing his chin then turning her attention back to her bowl of cereal. She scooped a spoonful of milk and bran flakes into her mouth as she leaned against the counter.

'Professional?'

'Very. But not too much.'

Jack smiled and stood a little straighter.

'Why wasn't I to be late again?'

'Because Gail and Alisha are dropping by for food tonight, remember?'

'Oh right. I remember you telling me now.'

'Do you?'

'Of course.'

Jack was pretty sure he had gotten away with that white lie.

Amy could tell by the way he wrung his hands together that he was lying.

She smiled and wondered if it was possible to love him any more than she already did.

'Any special occasion?' asked Jack, searching for his car keys.

'Honeymoon pictures.'

Jack straightened sharply, brow creased, 'Oh no, how many?'

'Stacks.'

'Right.' Jack got back to searching for his car keys. 'And you're quite sure I can't be late?'

'Turn up late and you're a dead man.'

'Roger Wilco.'

Jack found his keys on the key hook fixed to the wall, exactly where he always left them. He twirled them around his index finger as he pondered the night's coming attraction. Did the pleasure of their company over food and wine outweigh the tedium of *oohing* and *ahhing* at hundreds of honeymoon pictures? He was pretty sure it didn't.

'Looking forward to it,' he said.

'Me neither, but what can you do?'

'Pretend there was a fire during the night and the place is completely gutted?'

Amy raised an eyebrow and pursed her lips.

'Then tonight it is.'

Jack kissed her and then Jack said goodbye and then Jack was gone.

———

He could have sworn it was the next right, then the next left, then on until the roundabout, but now here he was, driving down a road he didn't recognise and the sky looked all wrong. It had a strange sepia tint to it, like an old photograph.

'Bugger.'

Jack's meeting two towns over had dragged on and he was now in a rush to get home. He thought he'd driven back the same way he'd travelled earlier, but found himself driving up and down country lanes he didn't recognise and of course the sat-nav had decided to go on the fritz.

There were no signposts, no other cars in sight, so he decided the very best thing to do would be to turn around and retrace his steps. Sixteen minutes later he realised with a heavy heart that he was as lost as he had ever been.

He pulled to a stop and checked his phone again but found it still had a stubborn lack of signal. Jack swore and struck the steering wheel with the palms of his hands. He was late. He'd promised he'd be back home in time and now he was late and getting later.

It was then he saw the house.

Jack had not noticed the house until that moment, which seemed altogether impossible as it was so large and situated directly in front him. How had he not seen it? There were no other buildings along this road that he could see; indeed he didn't believe he'd passed so much as a garage or a bus stop ever since he'd found himself where he didn't want to be.

Jack got out of his car and strode toward the front door. The house looked very old. Withered vegetation clung to much of the crumbling brick frontage, and several of the upstairs windows sported jagged cracks. If this had been a movie, then it would be exactly the kind of house the main character should definitely not approach, but always would.

'Probably abandoned,' said Jack to himself as he *knock-knock-knocked* the front door and disturbed a tsunami of dust. He waited, but there was no response. Jack gave it one last knock and then, just as he was about to turn and make his way back to his car, the door opened and revealed a man in a rabbit mask.

'Oh,' said Jack, which was a reasonable response.

The mask encased the man's head and had two large ears stretching upward. The mask was not plastic or rubber, it seemed solid and was covered with real (if tatty and aged) fur. Strange rabbit mask aside, the man wore an old suit of the sort that might have been fashionable when his great, great, grandfather was young.

'Hello,' said the man in the rabbit mask.

'Hello,' said Jack.

'Do you like my mask?'

'Yes, it's....nice?' he replied, even though the mask did not look 'nice' at all. It looked ratty and as though it very probably smelled. The man smiled and stroked his large ears. Jack did not know how he knew that the man had smiled, but he did.

'It was my mothers, fathers, mothers once upon a time, when the mountains were small and the seas were song, or so the story goes. For a time it was lost to us, but I found it where I thought I would, in the forest, under a tree, and I dug, dug, dug it up.'

As the man spoke, Jack felt a strange upside-down sensation in his stomach, which he put down to his worry at being so lost.

'Now Jack, how may I help?' asked the man.

'I wondered if....wait, how do you know my name?'

'You do look a lot like a Jack.'

'Do I?'

'Yes, and I look just how you'd expect a Mr. Cotton to look.'

'Well, yes...I suppose you do. Are you going to a fancy dress party?'

'Oh, at some stage, it's more than likely,' replied Mr. Cotton, and his large ears twitched. Jack ignored that because of course the ears were just part of a tatty old mask and so could not have twitched at all.

'I'm sorry to bother you, it's just I don't seem to know where I am and my phone isn't getting a signal. D'you think you could direct me back to the main road? I'm sure I could find my way again from there.'

'You would like to be put on the correct path?' asked Mr. Cotton.

'Yes please, I'm running late and haven't a clue as to where I've got to. Daft of me really, I don't know what happened, must have been daydreaming and taken a wrong turn or something.'

'So many wrong turns lurk where the right turn might be,' said Mr. Cotton, nodding.

'Yeah, I suppose that's...so those directions...?'

'Directions, yes. Turning right from wrong and on till bedtime.' Mr. Cotton clapped his white-gloved hands together and dust exploded, like a teacher slapping their chalk duster against the wall. 'I believe I would like to help, and I believe I will. My brother would also like to help.'

'Great! That'd be really very nice of you.'

'Good. Do you accept our help?'

'Sorry?'

'Jack, do you accept mine and my brothers' help?'

Jack wondered who Mr. Cotton's brother was. 'Oh. Sure. Thanks.'

'Good. Then we shall set you upon the path and what will be must be.' Mr Cotton's ears twitched once more, though of course they did not as it was just a mask.

———

Jack knew he must have been a long way from home after he drove away from Mr Cotton's house, but he found himself pulling up in front of his own house in less than ten minutes anyway.

'Amy? Amy, are you home?' asked Jack as he stepped across the threshold and closed the door behind him.

'Yes,' replied Amy, her voice creeping through from the other side of the house.

'Oh God, I know I'm late, I'm sorry, and my bloody phone wouldn't get a bloody signal so I couldn't even bloody send you a message or anything!' Jack plopped his coat onto the couch and stretched out a shoulder kink.

'That's fine,' said Amy.

'I'm just glad to be home at last. Listen, d'you mind if we cancel this thing with Gail and Alisha? I'm feeling a bit wonky, just want to flop in front of the telly all night.'

'Okay,' said Amy.

Jack couldn't believe his luck. He grabbed the remote control and flicked on the TV set; static greeted him. 'Balls,' Jack pressed another channel, more static. 'Amy, is the telly broken?'

'No,' said Amy. 'Everything is fine, fine, fine.'

Jack felt prickles race across his skin as he went from channel to channel. Finally he discovered a channel that was working. On screen was a close-up of what looked like a hedgehog mask.

'Oh,' said Jack. 'That's weird.'

'Is it? I'm sure it's not. I'm sure everything is fine, fine, fine.'

Jack got down onto his knees on the carpet and shuffled forward, peering closer at the hedgehog mask. It seemed to him that its wearer was watching him back, which, of course, was impossible.

Jack could hear the person breathing.

In and *out*

In and *out*

Raspy harsh against the mask. Just like the rabbit mask, it seemed old and ragged. Jack had the strange fear that if he were to move any closer toward the screen, the hedgehog man would reach out and take hold of him.

'You shouldn't sit so close you know, you'll get square eyes,' said Amy, who had entered the room behind him.

'Amy, I don't think I like this TV channel,' said Jack.

'No, it's fine. It's really fine, fine, fine.'

Jack turned from the screen to look up at his girlfriend, who smiled down at him. It was an odd sort of smile, Jack thought, more like she was showing off her teeth than a true smile. But that wasn't the oddest thing about Amy. No, the oddest thing was that she didn't have any eyes, and birds had taken up home inside her head, their small, sharp beaks poking out of Amy's empty sockets.

Jack was not the sort of man who screamed at scary sights or ghoulish frights, but even so, as he looked up at his eyeless girlfriend with her head full of birds, he found himself unleashing a small groan of horror.

'Oh, I enjoy this show,' said Amy, pointing to the hedgehog masked stranger on screen. 'Do I? I think I do. I'm sure I've seen it before and before and before.'

As he listened to Amy talk, Jack realised she didn't sound much like his girlfriend at all. The voice was too flat, empty of any colour or nuance. It was like someone had hollowed out her voice, and if he were to poke one of the words with his finger as she spoke them, it would collapse in on itself.

'Who are you?' he asked.

'Jack? I am Amy. Amy your girlfriend. We have dated for years and years and rent this house at a reasonable cost, all things considered. Shall we kiss?'

'No thanks.'

'Okay,' said Amy, and she dug into her pocket, retrieving a fist of soil full of fat, wiggling worms. 'Everything is fine, fine, fine.' She began to pull worms from the soil clump and held them before her eye sockets, the beaks snapping hungrily, until one found its target and pulled the worm from her fingers and into her head.

Jack wondered how she could see him with her eye sockets full of beaks. How could she think at all with a skull stuffed with feathers and claws and sharp, hungry squawks. He stood and began to edge away from Other Amy, as he now thought of her. Other Amy with her dead voice and starving beak eyes.

'Where are you going?' asked Other Amy, feeding fat worm after fat worm to the snapping beaks.

'Nowhere, I'm not going anywhere,' he replied, still edging around the room, shuffling slowly towards the door. Other Amy gazed once more at the TV set.

'Ah yes, I do remember this show, I knew I did. This is the *Mr. Spike Show*. Mr. Spike is funny, you know. Or terrifying. Or silly. Something along those lines.'

Jack found himself three steps from the door, his eyes never leaving Other Amy as she stood transfixed by the person in the mouldy hedgehog mask.

'Once I met Mr. Spike on a road that didn't exist. He took off his mask and I pulled out my eyes so as not to see what was shown. I can laugh about it now, you know. Everything is funny, given enough time.'

Jack reached out a hand and wrapped his fingers around the door handle, turning it slowly in the hope of silencing its rusty squeak.

'You going out then?' said Other Amy without turning to him.

'Yes, I...I think I left something in my car.'

'Oh yes? I expect it'll be there. It'll be right there where you expect, everything always is you see, because everything is fine, fine, fine.'

A beak pierced the back of Other Amy's skull and wiggled and fought until the bird's entire head poked through, slick with gore, and stared at Jack with black, glass eyes.

———

'Still no word on Jack?' asked Sonya.

Still thought Amy.

Still no word.

There had been no word—

No word at all—

And there still hadn't been.

Still wouldn't be.

Still couldn't be.

The world had opened up and Jack was *still* gone—

And gone—

And gone—

'No. Nothing new,' replied Amy.

Still nothing new.

That persistent lack of Jack sat heavy in her chest and her stomach and her everything; day after day after hour after minute after second.

Should the pressure of it have lessened even a little by now? Days had gone by—

—a week in fact, she suddenly realised, and then had to dig her nails into her palms to stop a horrid sort of wailing noise from seeping out of her mouth, slithering around the room, and scaring Sonya away.

No. That weight, that pressure, that ravenous consuming fuzzy bleak was still there. She wondered if it was just part of her now. If she'd traded Jack for this. This void. This empty that wasn't empty at all because if you reached your hand into the 'empty' you'd feel all the screaming and the terror and the anger and the 2 a.m. tears.

'How are you coping? *Are* you coping? Daft question. Sorry. It's the kind of question you ask though, isn't it? I mean, in a situation like this?'

'A situation like this?'

'Yeah. Well. Not like this. Not exactly like this because we don't know if he's... I mean... They haven't found a... ' Sonya trailed off and picked at the skin around her nails. 'Have you got any biscuits?'

'Yeah,' replied Amy. 'I think so. Let me have a look.'

She got up and went into the kitchen. She didn't actually look for biscuits, instead she bent over, rested her head in the sink, and listened to the tears *drip-drip-dripp*ing down the plughole.

'I'd best be off,' said Sonya.

'Okay then,' said Amy, her voice bouncing around her metal sink cocoon. 'Thanks so much for coming. Mind how you go. I'll call you in a few days. Might be cold out. Or hot. You never can tell. Don't let the bedbugs bite.'

It was dark, so a few hours must have slipped past unnoticed.

'We found a car.' That's what the police had said.

'Is it his? Is it Jack's?'

'Yes.'

'Where is he?'

'The car was found abandoned at the side of the road, several miles out of town on a country lane, the front end partially within an overgrown bush.'

'Jack? Where is he?'

'Well, he was not within the car. We checked. And he was not in or around the bush. Our best working theory is that he had an accident and perhaps bashed his skull against the steering wheel.'

'Though there is no physical evidence of that,' said the second officer.

'May I continue?' asked the first. The second gestured with one hand and the first nodded. 'So. Perhaps he did or didn't knock his head after coming to an unexpected halt, upon and after which, in a daze, perhaps with his senses and knowledge of himself knocked clean out of him, he left the car and took off on foot, to areas and places currently mysterious.'

'Was he a drinker,' asked the second.

'No. Well, yes. He drank.'

'I see,' said the first, and the officers exchanged glances.

'But he didn't drink and drive, if that's what you think.'

'We think nothing.'

'Nothing at all.'

'Not our place to think.'

'He was very careful about that sort of thing,' said Amy. 'He'd never drink and then get behind the wheel.'

The officers nodded.

'He may also have been forcibly abducted and or murdered.'

'Always a possibility.'

'Can't rule it out.'

'Won't rule it out.'

'Strange things can happen, outside the walls of a city.'

'It's an odd place out there.'

'Odd people.'

'All that grass and wide open spaces.'

'Well, it's not natural, is it?'

Maybe he'd just left her. You heard about that sort of thing. About someone just dropping out of their life. Ghosting. Hidden stresses and strains that one day just become too heavy to bear, so off they go, and never a word is heard.

But that didn't seem like Jack to Amy.

Jack loved her.

And she loved him.

He never would.

Wouldn't run away without a word.

Something had taken him from her and she knew it could be nothing good.

Amy sat at the bottom of the stairs and wondered how long it had been since she'd cleaned the bathroom.

Sometimes exhaustion overtook her and she'd sleep for hours and hours. Sometimes she felt so alert she walked the rooms of her house for days, yelling. The night was long and fearsome when your eyes refused to stay closed. It pressed in at you until you thought your head might split open from the pressure.

She had to get out.

So she put on her shoes, and she put on her coat, and she left the house.

As she drove, Amy felt as though she was dreaming. Like the world had gone soft and she was trapped inside one of her nightmares. Maybe that's all this was after all and she just had to find a way to wake up. She'd open her eyes and find Jack beside her, drooling on the pillow.

Or perhaps she'd gone mad.

It was all very strange and unreal and it made Amy feel wonky, as though her organs were bashing into each other like pinballs. Going mad had always been one of her greatest fears. Some yelped at spiders scuttling, others trembled deep down at the very idea of travelling by aeroplane, but the worry that snuggled Amy in her darker moments was the fear of losing her marbles.

'Who are you, then?' Granddad Thomas would say when she went to visit him in those final few years.

'It's me Granddad, Amy, your granddaughter,' she would reply, softly.

'Oh? Oh no. No, I don't think so, love. I'm only twenty-two, I haven't even had kids yet,' and he would look down at his wrinkled, brown-speckled hands in confusion.

'You're not mad, I'm sorry to say,' said a man sitting in the back seat of the car. 'You're quite sane, which is much, much worse.'

The man who was speaking wore a faded old suit.

Dusty white gloves.

And a rabbit mask.

A rabbit mask that began to stretch as a smile spread impossibly across it.

The wheel turned sharply and the car tyres screamed in complaint as the world lurched round and round, until things came to a sudden stop. Amy bashed her head and things turned to fuzz and sparks. She fumbled at the seat belt with rubber fingers, pushed open the door, and stumbled out of the car. Her hands scuffed the ground as she made her escape, painting the tarmac red.

Amy had felt scared many times in her life.

There was the time when she was six at the local swimming pool. She thought she knew what she was doing, but soon enough she'd walked too far and under she went, and there was no way she'd be able to get above the water again to catch her breath—

There were the times in class when the teacher was going from pupil to pupil and she knew she was going to have to stand and speak in front of everyone and her mouth was so, so dry and her heart was fluttering—

There was the time she climbed over a fence to retrieve a ball, and just as she'd found it and picked it up she'd heard a low growl and turned to see the biggest dog that had ever been, and the fence was too far away and there was no way she was going to make it but she turned to run anyway—

But this wasn't like that, this was a deep-down terror, primal and old and undeniable. It was *other* and it was *wrong* and it was *inevitable.*

Amy felt like curling up into a ball and crying.

Instead, she ran.

Ran down empty midnight streets, ran with eyes unblinking, ran until she had to stop because her body couldn't manage another step. Half crouching, half falling, she reached out to cushion the blow as she dropped to the ground and tore at the air with great, ragged breaths.

'There you are. I've been waiting for you.'

She looked up to see the man in the rabbit mask standing before her.

'My name is Mr. Cotton, and this is my dear brother, Mr. Spike.'

A second man stepped out of nothing. He wore a tatty hedgehog mask. His shoulders shuddered and a noise like twisting metal escaped from behind the mask. Amy believed it was the sound of his laughter.

'Now, do not be rude, Amy. Say hello to my brother, won't you?'

Amy tried not to. She tried to close her eyes tight. Tried to curl up and cover her head with her arms.

'Hello, Mr Spike.'

'There, now isn't that better?' replied Mr Cotton.

Amy thought about the first time she met Jack. About his eyes and his smile.

And then Mr Spike removed his mask.

***

Someone was knocking at the front door.

Amy looked around in confusion. She was sitting at the foot of the stairs. She was alone.

She'd been dreaming.

Must have been.

She had her shoes on, her coat, too, and in one hand she held her car keys.

Her hands were raw; dirt and dried blood. She decided to ignore that, because she'd just been dreaming after all.

Amy stood and shuffled forward, stopping by the mirror on the wall. The woman she saw looking back had wide, mad eyes and insane hair. Was that what she looked like now? She smiled and the reflection smiled back. It was a loon's smile that she'd never seen herself make before.

Oh yes, someone was knocking at the door.

Maybe it was the police. They'd found Jack's body. He'd been taken to an abandoned caravan and tortured for days. A passing rambler had been alerted by the reek of his corpse seeping out into the field.

Amy opened the door.

Jack was waiting.

He smiled and his eyes were big and vulnerable and hazel, just like she remembered.

'Hello, Jack,' she said.

'Hello, Amy,' he replied. 'Sorry I'm late.'

She threw her arms around him.

She kissed his neck, his cheek, his shoulder.

She hugged him so tight it was a wonder that his ribs didn't crack.

That his eyes didn't bulge from their sockets.

That his heart didn't pop like a water balloon.

'I knew you'd come back,' she said. 'I love you so much.'

'I love you, too,' replied Jack.

'I think I've been having the most terrible of nightmares.'

'Oh dear.'

'But now I'm awake and you're here and everything is going to be okay.'

Jack did not reply.

'It is going to be okay, isn't it?'

'Of course,' said Jack. 'Everything is fine, fine, fine.'

AUTHOR BIO

Matthew Stott is an author and publisher and has written for BBC television and radio. His novels include the middle-grade books *A Monstrous Place*, *The Identical Boy*, and *The Increasingly Transparent Girl*, and the urban fantasy series *Hexed Detective*. Find him on Twitter: @MattStottWrites

Mycelium Ouroboros

by Nikki R. Leigh

Field Note, December 17th, 2009

Location: No way I'm telling you, but just so I know: it's that place near the trees that look a bit like your Aunt Helen and her husband.

The forest is screaming today.

Birds, loud and angry that I'm trampling deep into the folds of their homes, the air hot despite the incoming Winter. I am not to be deterred though. The ground is soft, the hairs on my arm are standing tall, pointing me up and away from the forest floor where I should be scouting.

These truffles won't find themselves, you know?

In all my years hunting the decadent fungus, I haven't hit it big yet. But I know I can do it. I'm capable. I don't need a dog or a pig. I have me, and my sensibility.

This is my year. My harvest. I'm here to fill my bags with expensive dirt.

If I have to rake this forest empty, I will.

And maybe that's why the woods are screaming today. The metal rake is firm in my hands, and I can hear the birds calling out my treason. It's like they're yelling "Josie, Josie, you know that what you're about to do will wreck the floor of these woods for cycles to come. Be less destructive, Josie. Do it for Hannah, Josie."

How they know the name of my wife is beyond me, but that's what I'm convinced they're yelling. But like I said before, I won't be deterred.

The teeth of my rake digs into the dirt, and I can almost hear the roots of trees and ferns and bushes groaning and snapping against the metal prongs. The resistance only makes me dig deeper, hoping to grab the delectable fungus in the mouth of the rake.

I can cover more ground this way. Make my days shorter. And no one cares but the forest, and she can't really talk so I'm going to plow until I can make my $300 for the day.

The birds continue to scream. I continue to hunt. The sun begins to set. I'll be back tomorrow.

———

Field Note, December 19th, 2009

Location: Half mile North from Aunt Helen and her husband. Look for the rock that smells like shit.

I didn't write yesterday because my hands were too raw from the raking. The skin still burns and stings today, but I have to document what I just found.

I'd raised the earth of nearly a football field worth of forest floor. The days only churned a handful of worthwhile fungus. None of the best stuff, but something at least to keep the wolves at bay so that the bills get paid, and Hannah can stay at home and write her book for a little while longer.

But about five minutes ago, I found it. It sat in a spotlight of yellow rays, filtered through the dense thicket of trees like a goddamned scene from a fairytale. Glimmering under the sun, the ring appeared.

A ring of mushrooms, more precisely.

I don't see them often. In fact, I haven't seen them at all in this stretch of the woods, now that I think about it. Not in this forest, where the fog lays dense during the day and the birds scream obscenities at you.

These woods, that I thought would yield the truffles I needed because, let's face it, they looked haunted as shit. So haunted that I didn't think other people would come out here and all the unearthed bundles of fungal gold would be mine.

No one wants to rupture the earth in a haunted forest. No one wants to disturb that soil. So yeah, the fog, the bird screams, the distinct lack of people—

And now, a fairy ring of mushrooms.

All the truffle hunting science points to these circles of mushrooms as being indicative of lush soil, ripe with truffles. You see 'em, you start digging.

So I did. I examined the three-yard diameter, followed the circumference of the circle, closed my eyes and started the search. Tried to sniff out the rich scent I told myself I could detect. Put my arms out like a dowsing rod.

And there, at the center, I clawed the dirt away from mid-point of the circle and unearthed perfect lumps of dirt...

Truffles. Rotted to the core.

The birds laughed at me.

I laughed back, throwing fetid truffles at the trees.

As the brown shapes arced across the sky, I could see the darkness creeping in.

The only thing worse than a haunted forest is being in one at night. Even I'm not brave enough for that.

Field Note, December 20th, 2009

Location: Back at that godforsaken rock.

I found the spot I left yesterday. Followed the lines I'd dragged in the dirt with my metal rake to lead me back the next day.

I had a bone to pick with this part of the forest.

I had truffles to force from the earth.

The woods aren't *really* haunted, you know. Don't want to mislead my notes here with my hyperbolic take of the creeping eyes of the forest and my overblown courage. I don't actually think there are ghosts here.

But the trees, this dirt, and most specifically, this fairy ring has haunted my thoughts all night, to be sure. Called me back with a whispering, slithering voice.

Hannah had asked how things were going, her eyes red from hours spent at the computer. I lied and told her I was going to strike it big. I stood, guilt in my throat like a knot in a log.

I'm back at this fairy ring today to make it bleed. Make it weep with truffles. Make it undo my lie, make it a truth.

I've spent the last hour searching the soil around the ring, my nose practically to the dirt. The birds are laughing, I know, at my ass pointed skyward. I've given them the finger several times already, but it hasn't shut them up.

My frustration is mounting, and it's taking all my will not to break my rake over this goddamned ring of mushrooms, their rounded tips pointing at me, like kids in a classroom who've found their mark to ridicule.

A blister on my hand pops, and so does my ability to contain myself. I step to the center of the ring, and I start wailing on these assholes, these laughing fungi.

I swing and bash and my arms start to buckle and I look at my destruction and see the chunks of white mushrooms scattered about. No longer a ring. Just pieces of trash on a trash floor of a trash forest.

I throw my rake on the floor.

I leave.

———

*Field Note, December 21*st*, 2009*

Location: Rock.

I tried to forget the ring, but I needed to go back. It sang circles of rot in my brain all night. Hannah had to repeat herself several times to be heard over the cacophony of fungal hymns in my head.

I had to come back. Plus, I left my rake in the spot, and I *really* like that rake and I can't afford another anyway. So here I am, at the scene of my destruction except it's not destruction anymore.

Where once dozens of mushrooms lay broken like little bastards on the floor of the forest, the circle has returned. Fuller than before.

I rub my eyes, then chide myself for touching my face with my dirt-ridden hands.

I blink.

The ring is still there, right next to my rake which had ripped the circle to shreds the day before.

Maybe the forest is haunted after all.

I shake myself from my stupor, reach forward to grab my rake at the center of the mushroom ring. I cross the threshold.

I don't cross it again.

I'm still here, stuck in the center of the ring with my notebook, my pen, and my rake, and it's all I can do to document what happens in case someone follows those lines to my place in the woods.

But the change is already taking place, so I'm not sure how much good it will do.

My feet are rooted to the center, my shoes flush against the earth. About thirty minutes ago, I felt a tingling in my soles, then a worming of flesh through the rubber of my shoes digging deep into the soil. I screamed and the birds laughed back at me.

It took a bit to regain my composure. No matter how hard I pulled against the ground, my feet wouldn't move from their spots, like they'd become a part of an ancient root structure. And to try and tear away felt like it was ripping tendons from my muscles and bones. I was pulled taut, snapping back to the ground.

The woods are crying for my blood, just as I had tried to bleed it dry. The ring of mushrooms have travelled from their place around me, diving under me, through me.

I'm becoming it. The fungus. The ring feeding on itself. Feeding me. Pulling me through it and back out to the ring. It stands taller than it did before.

I can feel the change climbing up my legs, up my torso, and I begin to cry when it reaches my chest. I lift my shirt, seeing the white rubbery tube I've become.

My body, a mushroom stalk.

My neck, fast turning into the gills, my skin structured mycelium.

I've been like this for another ten minutes.

My body burns and all I can think about is how I'm becoming death. How I'm becoming a part of the decomposition chain.

How I'm becoming the very thing I hunt: a treasure in the soil. I vaguely consider that my bones will not be worth their weight in truffles. No time to write more. Tell you how much this hurts.

I can smell myself rot.

Arms are tubes. Pen is heavy. Brain is fuzzy. Eyes dark.

I hope that Hannah finishes her book.

Field notes from the notebook of Josie Danielson. Found by Park Ranger Dylan. To be filed with Ms. Danielson's Missing Persons Report. Park Ranger Dylan includes the following notes with his report and this notebook:

"When I arrived at the site, I saw the forest floor had been raked recently, presumably by the metal rake found near the notebook of Josie Danielson. Ms. Danielson was nowhere to be found. No footsteps led away from the site. Other items

gathered included a pile of clothing, recently worn and a bag half-filled with various types of fungi.

What I'm about to include in this report is odd, but I want to be diligent. I hope that any information might lead to Ms. Danielson's return. Perhaps someone in the area is selling what I'm about to describe.

Around the pile of clothes was a ring of mushrooms. White, flecked with some red. Haven't seen this species before, uniform in their growth. The most remarkable thing, how they stood almost at attention. A plump bottom, small tubes dangling from their gills. A second lump on top. Two more tubes flopping from their sides. Humanoid in their shape.

I took a sample, which I have bagged to be filed with this report.

There was no sign of a struggle."

AUTHOR BIO

Nikki R. Leigh is a queer, forever-90s-kid wallowing in all things horror. When not writing horror fiction and poetry, she can be found creating custom horror-inspired toys, making comics, and hunting vintage paperbacks. She reads her stories to her partner and her cat, one of which gets scared very easily. Instagram - @spinetinglers Twitter - @fivexxfive

Justine

by Gemma Amor

(Content Warning: Rape)

Justine is angry.

Her trembling fingers are white, gripping her cellphone with tremendous force. A placatory voice oozes out of the phone speaker, cooing gentle, conciliatory words that are meant to soften the devastating blow they convey.

'I'm sorry, Justine,' the voice says. It is Michael, her lawyer. 'I really am. I know how much tomorrow meant to you.'

But Justine cannot hear it. All she can hear is the loud rushing noise that has taken over the space between her ears. All she can think is one thing, over and over again, as her whole body locks tight with white, hot, suppressed rage.

Coward, she thinks.

Coward, coward, coward!

The voice on the phone continues.

'They found him in his cell early this morning. He...uhhh, wow, how do I say this?' Michael sighs heavily. Justine can hear him scratching his head with the end of his pen.

'He hung himself with his own jumpsuit, Justine. Twisted it into a rope and looped it around...well, it doesn't really matter *how*, does it?' Michael clears his throat. 'All that matters is that Uriah is dead. But at least...'

'Don't say it.' Justine interrupts, furiously. 'Just...don't...say it!'

'I'm trying to find the silver lining here, Justine,' the voice continues, regardless. 'At least he can't hurt anyone anymore. There is a sort of justice in that, at least.'

Justice? She thinks, and the rushing noise intensifies.

No!

No, there isn't!

She swallows, fighting back bitter tears, hating the man on the other end of the phone.

'I wanted him to stand trial, Michael,' she manages, eventually. Thick, sour spittle has built up inside her cheeks. Her head begins to pound and throb, and her breath hitches, coming fast and shallow. The rushing sound becomes a rising wall of white noise that presses in on her, threatens to crush her under its weight. Her chest heaves and subsides as if she is running a race: a panic attack is thundering towards her at breakneck speed.

'Justine?' Her mother is suddenly there, prising the phone from her hands, steering her towards the couch, pushing her down gently into a sitting position. Michael's voice calls out in miniature from the cellphone. Justine's mother jabs her finger at the screen, hangs up on him, throws the phone across the room. She sits next to Justine, gently rubbing her back, encouraging her to breathe slowly, mumbling gentle nonsense words of comfort, holding back her own tears.

But it is no good. The panic attack seizes hold of Justine and she begins to rock, backwards and forwards on the spot, and then to clutch at the air, and then to beat herself around the temples with her fists. Her Mother, who has grown used to these attacks, tries to catch Justine's fists with her own hands, and restrain her, but fails on both counts: she is only a little woman. Justine rains fierce, violent blows down upon her own, tired head, and her Mother sits next to her, waiting. Best to just ride it out, offer what little comfort she can.

Eventually, the attack passes. Justine stops struggling, and begins to cry, exhausted, defeated, cheated of the means by which to do what everyone tells her she needs to do: 'move on'.

There will be no 'moving on'.

The man who hurt her was supposed to stand trial.

The man who hurt her was supposed to be punished in a court of law.

The man who hurt her...is...

Dead.

'Uriah killed himself,' she says, eventually, when the breath seeps slowly back into her burning lungs, by way of explanation. Her mother's eyes grow wide with horror.

'No!' she exhales, and again, 'Oh, *no*,' and Justine breaks down for the second time.

Court. He is supposed to be in court, tomorrow. He is supposed to stand before her while he is charged with seven counts of rape, one count of kidnapping and imprisonment, and one count of attempted murder. He is supposed to stand there and face a jury, face a judge, and ultimately, importantly, vitally, he is supposed to face *her*.

Justice.

Instead, he has cheated her, one last time. He has killed himself, so that she can never get the closure she needs.

She imagines him smiling as he winds the makeshift noose around his neck. She imagines his last feelings of triumph and he squeezes the life out of his own body. She imagines his dead corpse, bug-eyed, and bloated, foam leaking out of the corner of his mouth, and she knows he has gone beyond her reach.

And Justine is suddenly, overwhelmingly, blindingly angry.

Because Uriah Dice has cheated her.

———

Justine attends Uriah's funeral.

She wears a disguise for the occasion: a long, blonde wig, a baseball cap, dark sunglasses and a black sports jacket. She finds a remote spot under a yew tree in the cemetery and waits, and watches, from a distance, afraid that she will be recognised. She needn't have bothered. There aren't many people in attendance. A pastor, and an old woman she can only assume is the Uriah Dice's mother. She finds it hard to believe that he ever had a mother, that he was ever raised from a child to a man like other, normal people were. The old woman is frail, and brow-beaten. She doesn't raise her head as the pastor reads from his bible. She doesn't lay flowers on the coffin, or throw a handful of earth. She waits patiently for the service to conclude, waits as if bearing a heavy load, and when the words are read, and the soil shovelled back into the hole in the ground, she simply turns, and walks away, and does not look back. Justine may have had it in her once to feel sympathy for the woman, to empathise with her heartbreak, but not now.

Not now.

Justine waits for the gravediggers and the pastor to leave the cemetery. The light is failing when she is finally left alone. She removes her cap, her wig, her sunglasses- there is no need for a disguise. She walks slowly between the headstones, laying a hand on this one, or that one, feeling cool marble and scratchy green lichen under her fingertips. *This is too nice a resting place for a piece of shit like Uriah Dice,* she thinks.

She reaches the freshly dug grave. She stands still, like an animal scenting the air at night, her whole body guitar-string taut, and looks down.

There is no headstone, only a wooden cross with a brass plaque. It bears a simple inscription:

Here lies
Uriah Dice
1963 - 2017

Justine hawks, and spits. The phlegm arcs in the air and lands on the freshly disturbed soil, and she is ashamed, momentarily, because she is stooping to his level, but then she remembers plastic zip ties cutting into her wrists and ankles, she remembers hot, foul breath on her face, she remembers pain, she remembers how he spat on her naked body after he had finished, every single time, like a ritual of some sort, as if she were a whore, or a dog, and that was his way of showing her this, expunging his own guilt somehow, and the shame melts away like snow before fire.

She rubs at the shiny, pink scars around her slender wrists and feels the full force of her hate and anguish coursing through every tiny capillary in her body. She feels as if it will shoot out of her feet and spread through the earth and put roots down far into the ground, and eventually, instead of a woman, there will be a bitter, black, twisted tree around which nothing will grow except poisoned ivy.

Why did I come here? Justine thinks, blinking back tears. *What good is this doing anyone?*

A voice speaks out from behind her.

'Do you have any spare change, madam?' It says, politely.

Justine starts and turns to see a man standing a few feet away, his figure largely obscured by a huge, shapeless, hooded jacket, the hood drawn up around his face so that she can only see suggestions of his features, not the whole. He leans heavily upon a long-handled shovel, watching her with shadowy, deep-set eyes. In his left hand he holds a fistful of long, thick ropes. Attached to the end of these are three large dogs, german shepherds, sitting patiently at his feet, panting fast, huge pink tongues dangling out of their mouths, hot breath making clouds of steam in the cool night air.

She frowns at him.

'You scared me,' she says, coldly. The man bows his head by way of apology. One of his dogs lets out a thin, anxious whine.

'I apologise,' he says, patting the dog's head to comfort it. Justine feels suddenly strange, cold, remote from herself: as if her body has emptied out, and there is only the skin left behind.

'What do you want?' she asks, dreamily, her voice floating out of her unbidden.

'No, Justine,' the man says, and his voice is suffused with an undertone of power, and dread, and there is a touch of sadness there, too. He continues, his face still wreathed in shadow.

'What do *you* want?'

'Me?' Inside her mind, where she has been suddenly locked away, Justine is beginning to question the events that are unfolding. Who is this man? Why is he talking to her? Why is she even listening to him? Why does she feel so... strange?

Why can't she...why doesn't she just... walk...away?

The scars on her wrists tingle and burn. She looks down, sees blood: bright, vital, crimson blood, arterial blood, dripping onto the earth from two long, deep cuts in her flesh, and dissolving into the ground.

'What is this?' she says, sleepily, and the dogs begin to whine, an anxious, high-pitched chorus.

'You are dead, Justine,' the man says, with a weary type of acceptance that speaks to his experience in the matters.

Justine remembers.

She *is* dead.

She ended things, hours after finding out that the man who kidnapped, used and kept her in a broken down concrete bunker in the woods for days on end had hung himself, rather than face trial.

But there is more to it than that, she muses as the memories of her own passing return. There had been a purpose in mind when she'd done it. The purpose eludes her at this precise moment, and so she stands, dead, above the grave of Uriah Dice, and shakes her head.

'Oh,' she says, unsure of what to do next.

The man in the hooded jacket holds out his free hand, a universally recognised symbol for payment.

'Got any spare change?' He says, for the second time, and things start to click into place for Justine. A line from an old song her Dad used to like swims through her memories:

"Don't pay the ferryman,

Don't even fix a price,
Don't pay the ferryman,
Until he gets you to the other side..."
The Ferryman.

She has studied Greek mythology at school. *Don't pay the Ferryman,* the song says...The Ferryman of the dead. A single coin, payment for taking dead souls across the River Styx and into the underworld. What happens to those who do not pay? She tries to remember, buries herself deep into her sixteen-year-old, expensive, private school curriculum, and eventually, it comes to her: those who do not pay to get to the underworld become ghosts, miserable, homeless, doomed to wander for eternity.

She looks down at Uriah Dice's grave.

'Did he pay the fee, too?' she asks, gesturing at the heap of earth. An idea of why she was dead is beginning to coalesce, crystalize in her mind. She would not have killed herself unless there had been an intention attached to it. She had been too angry for that. She had survived too much, clung to life too stubbornly in that bunker to collapse in on herself now and give up the fight.

The Ferryman nodded. 'Uriah paid his penny,' he confirms.

'Right.' Justine smiles, suddenly. 'So Uriah is, what? In the underworld? In hell?'

The Ferryman is silent, watchful. Justine takes his silence as confirmation, and her smile grows wider. She fumbles in her pockets, and eventually, her cold fingers find a single, lonely coin. She doesn't know how it got there, but that hardly matters. She offers it to the man. He loops the dog leashes around his wrist to free up a hand, which he then extends. It is bony, hideously bony, the hand of a skeleton thinly wrapped in papery skin, but for some reason Justine is not afraid. She can't see the Ferryman's face, but she knows he is smiling, somehow.

The coin drops. His skeletal fingers close around it, and somewhere, a bell tolls, announcing what feels like a new contract. The air about them seems to shimmer. For a moment, she sees water, hears the sound of waves lapping against the side of a boat. The shovel in the man's hands no longer looks like a shovel, but a long, wooden oar, and they are standing in the boat together, moving along a river, and she looks down, into the water, which churns with unnatural movement, and she sees faces, thousands of tormented, twisted, blackened faces, mouths open, drowning, and she sees other things in the water, slithering, scabrous forms, scales, teeth, and all of it...

All of it is chaos.

And then she blinks, and the river has gone, and the man is just a man again, a man with three dogs and a shovel, which he holds out to her. Justine accepts it. The shovel is heavy, and she almost drops it, then tightens her grip, determined. The Ferryman extends a single, bony finger, points at the grave behind her.

Justine turns, looks down. *Here lies Uriah Dice*, she thinks.

But not for long.

She drops the shovel blade smartly on the heaped soil of Dice's grave. She pauses for a moment, takes a deep breath, and jams her boot downwards, making a definitive, audible slice in the soil. Once the first cut it made, she feels suddenly better, set righteously upon a path that she has been searching for.

She starts digging, in earnest.

The Ferryman, payment received, walks away into the night. As he goes, Justine can hear his dogs, whining.

———

She digs for hours. It is hard, blistering work. Her hands are bloody and raw against the shovel handle. The earth is heavy, and difficult to move, despite it being freshly dug and turned over once already that day. She keeps going. She has purpose once again.

She hits wood just as she is on the verge of collapse. The shovel blade hits Dice's coffin with a resolute 'thunk!', sending a jolt of impact up both her arms. It reverberates around her chest, and makes her fingers tingle.

Reaching inside of herself, Justine finds a thin dreg of energy, and uses the shovel to lever off the coffin lid. It is empty, which she expected after her conversation with the Ferryman. Uriah is now in hell, after all. He paid his toll.

She peers in, struggling to see in the settling gloom, and realises that the coffin is not *completely* empty. Set into the white, unblemished silk lining of the coffin base is a single, round brass handle. It looks like a Victorian door knob. She wraps her sore hand around it, and tugs. A thin outline of blazing, bright light suddenly appears, as if someone has drawn it there with a pen in the shape of a door.

Uriah is behind that door, she is certain.

She heaves, and pulls the secret door open, hungry for her promised reunion. The light grows steadily brighter as the door cracks wider. She has a moment to reflect upon the absurdity of her situation, as she stands, six feet under the surface of the earth, legs braced on the sides of the coffin, earth and roots and worms and beetles all around, coated in mud and sweat and blood, a shovel gripped in one hand, a door handle in the other. A moment to wonder at her own lust for revenge, and then there is only light: cleansing, brilliant, awesome light, washing over her.

This is the mouth of hell, and Justine is going in.

Justine is going to find Uriah Dice.

Justine is going to bring him back.

Justine descends into the light.

Blinking, she waits for her vision to clear.

It is hot, unbearably so, and she is bathed in a sheen of sweat within moments of opening her eyes. An unnatural type of daylight floods every corner of her vision, so bright she can barely see. She uses her hands as shields, peers painfully through her fingers to try and get her bearings.

She finds herself in a valley. It is long, and winding, the sides of it steep with white chalky cliffs that are thickly papered with dead moss and parched, thin grass that hasn't seen water or shade for a very, very long time. The air smells of dust, and scorched, dead, burned things. Cicadas scream ceaselessly all around her, almost invisible except for tiny flickering movements on the cliffs here and there.

Justine stares for a moment, afraid of this placid scene, and then walks forward, cautiously. She has no preconceptions of what hell will be like. She is not a bible person, she does not remember much of what was taught to her when she was young. She knows that hell is where the bad people go, and that is enough for her. She knows that Uriah Dice is here, somewhere. That is the only important thing. Without fear, without much of anything except for a dull, constant, furious resolve that burns in the pit of her belly, she walks on, searching, searching.

It is unbearably hot, which she supposes she should have anticipated at the very least. Within moments, her throat is parched, and her lips begin to dry out, peel, crack under the blistering sun. She walks onwards, a thin trickle of blood snaking down her chin from a sudden split on her lower lip. She tongues at it absentmindedly, savouring the saltiness as she does so. The valley seems to stretch out endlessly before her in a straight, monotonous line, the chalk cliffs towering up above on both sides, but neither side offering any shade from the relentless, burning sun that fills the sky overhead.

She stops, sheds a layer of clothing, dragging her sports jacket up over her head, wrapping it around her hair to make a rough turban, trying to protect her scalp from the intense rays. She closes her eyelids as she does this, to give herself a moment's rest from the glare, and when she opens them again she gasps in fear.

There are bodies, lining the valley.

Floating in the air, suspended upside down, like maggots on a fishhook, mere feet away from her.

Thousands upon thousands of human bodies, row upon row, stretching out as far as her eyes can see.

They are horribly naked, and pale, almost white, and hairless. Their own eyes are closed, but their mouths hang open, slack, tongues lolling, thin trails of drool leaking out and spidering down to the ground. Their ankles are uniformly bound by great, iron chains. The chains climb up into the sky and disappear into the brilliant atmosphere above. Justine has a flashback to her own legs, savagely bound by zip ties, and slows her pace.

All is eerily quiet, other than the occasional chink and clank of the chains as they sway slowly in a non-existent breeze, and the buzzing sound of insects. Justine's breath catches in her throat. Blood streaks down the flanks and thighs and torsos of each body, and drips, pooling underneath, small, persistent rivulets of crimson winding their way past her feet and across the valley floor. Flies have amassed, and they swarm about erratically, drunk on blood and flesh. They gather on the faces of the hanged, crawl inside their open mouths and across their eyelids and around their genitals. *Looking for the softest parts*, she thinks.

Justine is afraid. She puts a single foot forward, tentative, wondering if she can make a run for it through the ranks of the hanged. As she does so, the body closest to her opens its eyes, and begins to wail, reaching out for her with thin, bloodied fingers. One by one, every single body jerks awake, in a terrifying, uncoordinated ripple of awareness, and Justine is surrounded by thousands of screeching, reaching figures,

hands outstretched, scrabbling for her, pulling her in. The noise crescendos, a hideous chorus of pain, and suffering, and the fingers are tearing at her clothes, and if she blinks she can see Uriah, tearing at her clothes, his fat red digits mutilating the expensive silk shirt she had worn that day, shredding through her lacy bra, mashing into the flesh that revealed itself beneath, and Justine does not want to relive this, does not want this memory to be her downfall, and so she does the only thing she can think to do. Rather than run through the sea of suspended bodies, she looks to the sky, and thinks one word:
Up.
She jumps, and clutches at one of the giant chains from which a body hangs, a maggot on a fishhook, wriggling and writhing and whipping about, and she puts her booted foot onto the thing's chin for a boost, ignoring the mad snapping of its teeth, and she hauls herself upwards, up past the clutching fingers, up past the bony, almost translucent abdomen, inside which she can see blackened intestines, moving about like twisting snakes, up past the pubis, up past the bony, swollen, pulpy knees, horrible, sticky blood soaking into her clothes and skin, and then she is on the chain, and the chain is a ladder, and she climbs, and climbs, and climbs, sobbing, into the vast wide blue above.

———

Justine met Uriah at work, or more specifically, at a work party. It had been one of those days, the project she was leading was horribly behind on schedule, feelings had run high, and books had been thrown. Her entire office was subsequently looking for an excuse to shed the memory of the preceding eight hours, and knuckle down to some serious recreational drinking.

Justine didn't normally drink, especially in front of her colleagues, but on that day, she had made an exception. Her company had hired the top floor of a private bar, and she had been given the company credit card. She knew why, as well: in two week's time, most of her team would be made redundant. They didn't know that yet, and this impromptu generosity on the part of their employers didn't seem to raise any suspicions, either. Free booze was free booze, and those on the receiving end of unexpected generosity were not prone to look the gift horse in the mouth.

Justine brandished the company card with great skill and dexterity, ordering in round after round, and she drank, and drank, and then drank some more. She became aware that she was behaving outrageously, flirting with a man easily ten years her junior. He looked half-terrified, half-turned on by her attentions, which made her clamp down on him even harder as the night progressed, desperate as she was to feel something other than this ever-present, vast burden of stress. Eventually, and somewhat inevitably, she found herself alone in the bar, the young man having made his own, drunken exit an hour earlier, with a wry smile and a worried look in his eyes. Rejected, and horribly depressed, Justine leaned her head against the bar counter and thought about closing her eyes, which were already drooping from fatigue. Doing so would only make the room spin, she knew, and when that happened, it was game over. She wanted to cling to some tiny vestige of dignity, even if it was attached to the small victory of leaving the bar without puking.

Don't close your eyes, stupid, she told herself, and so opened them again.

And saw Uriah, sidling up to her from a corner where he'd been sitting, and, she realised slowly through the booze, watching her.

He was a large man, in both height and girth. He had a round, prominent stomach that spilled over the waistband of his trousers and swayed when he walked. His face was fleshy, and flushed, although not in a healthy way, his features thick.

He smelled of beer and garlic and something else she couldn't identify, but was repulsed by, nonetheless. It was stale, musty. The kind of smell that permeated everything and didn't wash out. She shuddered thinking about his house, what kind of conditions he lived in.

Is this what I have come to? She thought to herself as Uriah approached, an eager look on his face. She adjusted her stance as best she could, standing more rigidly, trying to portray her unavailability.

No, thanks. I have some *standards, at least,* she thought.

Her body language didn't work. The large belly loomed into her peripheral, and his smell threatened to overwhelm her.

'Staying for another?' Uriah asked, and his voice, for such a large man, was curiously high-pitched.

'Not for me, I'm afraid,' said Justine, unsteadily, waving her credit card around in the vague hope it would summon the suddenly absent barman so she could settle the astronomical tab.

Uriah moved closer, and Justine began to gabble, her nerves getting the better of her. 'Uriah, is it?' she asked, her voice brittle with false politeness. 'You work in the mail room, don't you?'

Where the fuck is the fucking barman? Was all she could think.

Uriah ignored her.

'I really think you should stay,' he wheedled, and took another step closer.

'No, *thank* you,' Justine said, more firmly this time, although a panicky edge had crept into her voice, and she realised that this was not a good thing, because, incredibly, her fear was exciting him, and he moved closer still, his breath now hot and fast on her face. She tried to back away, an involuntary retching movement working her jaw, but he had managed to pin her against the bar with his vast bulk, and then, just as the thought registered that something was terribly wrong, just as his meaty hand began to reach for her right tit, just as she saw something bulge in his crotch and his mouth fall slack, she began to feel her stomach knot and her head pound and then, suddenly, vomit rose up her throat and she was sick, all over him, a watery, acrid puke that told a tale of too much vodka on an empty stomach. And, as time slowed in the aftermath, she locked eyes with him, and saw the shock, and the disappointment, and the revulsion as Uriah realised what had just happened, and she couldn't help herself. She did something she wished every day after that one for the rest of her life that she hadn't.

She laughed at him.

Eventually, Justine realises that she is no longer climbing. Which is good, because her arms and legs burn with effort, her muscles worn out. She finds herself lying on her back in tall grass, which sways and swishes around her in a cool breeze. Her skin pimples, but the temperature difference is welcome after the stifling heat of the valley from which she'd climbed. Exhausted, she is content to just lie there, catching her breath, until a single word starts pounding at her mind over and over again.

Uriah.

Uriah.

Uriah.

It doesn't matter how bad the remembering gets, she is here to do a job.

She rises to her feet.

And finds herself in a waiting room.

Justine saw Uriah around the office a few times after the vomiting incident, which she remembered vaguely and with a greasy sense of shame that meant she tried to stuff the memory as far to the back of her mind as possible. Uriah had other ideas. Rather than be repulsed by her behaviour, their horrible encounter that night seemed to spur him on, as if the contents of her stomach had been an invitation to proceed with courting instead of a declaration of disgust. He began bringing mail to her desk that didn't belong to her, and then, not long after, other things: notes, small gifts, his phone number on sticky post-it notes. She was too preoccupied with the first round of redundancies to pay it as much attention as he no doubt craved. His harassment of her should, under normal circumstances, have eaten away at her sense of security, but she was so rarely at her desk anymore that she often didn't get the notes and trinkets until the end of the day, when it was easy to swipe them off her desktop and into the trash basket and leave, without having to engage with them any further.

Meeting merged into meeting into meeting, until she felt as if her entire life was one never-ending meeting, a collection of people in a single room all staring at a PowerPoint presentation with watery eyes and dry mouths and tight foreheads. After the meetings, there would be drinks in the local bar, and after that, restless, unsatisfying sleep where she relived the stunned faces of her colleagues as she handed them their letters telling them to pack their things and go. The worst thing about all of this was that she was pretty sure she was next on the list to be given the boot. Having done all the dirty work of firing for them, the board were clearly gearing up for her own departure, and this felt like the biggest insult of all: thanks for all the redundancies, don't let the door bite you on the ass on the way out.

Eventually, the letter came, and with it, a strange sense of relief: she was exhausted, she was drinking too much, and she had hardly any friends left in the building now that she'd had to get rid of them all. In an odd way, getting fired was an opportunity to rest, take stock of her life, re-focus. Maybe she'd set up on her own as a consultant, like she'd always planned to do. She could make three times what she earned now, and that would enable her to save for that trip to Thailand she'd always wanted to take. Silver linings all around, if she thought about it. It was just a matter of swallowing her pride and moving on.

She packed her things wearily into a plastic crate and made her way down to the underground parking lot where her car was. As she moved through the office doors and made for the elevator, she saw the familiar lumbering shape of Uriah coming up the corridor towards her. She kept her eyes averted, but he drew closer, and then blocked her path with the mail cart. Her heart sank.

'You, too?' he said in his odd squeaky voice and pointed at her crate of belongings. There was something akin to panic in his eyes, which were a little too wide and round, his breathing a little too heavy.

'Yep,' she said, tiredness threatening to knock her down. She didn't need this, not right now. Uriah didn't make to move. 'I, ah...I need to get to my car,' she said, gesturing at him to move aside.

'But you can't leave,' Uriah said, ignoring her, his bulk as immovable as that of a mountain.

Justine shrugged. 'Take it up with management,' she said, her temper beginning to flare. 'Now, I really do need to get to my car. Would you mind moving, please?'

Uriah just stood, and stared at her, motionless. She stared back, a million different conflicting emotions racing through her. Then she sighed in exasperation, turned smartly on her heel, and retraced her steps, heading for the stairwell instead of the elevator. What was a few flights of stairs, really, if it meant finally escaping this place?

She heard the mail cart start to move, and then trundle along behind her, keeping pace as she walked. She didn't look back, but she could feel Uriah's eyes on her back, her ass, her legs. She sped up, her heels clopping on the sterile blue carpet, fluorescent strip lights beaming down from overhead, and the mailcart trundled louder, moved more quickly, to match her speed. Her plastic crate of stuff was heavy, or she would have broken into a jog, but thankfully, the door leading to the stairwell appeared on her left, just in time. She ducked through it, heart pounding in her chest, and stamped down the stairs as fast as she could without falling, down, down, down, away from Uriah.

When she finally got to her car she popped the trunk, threw her crate of things inside, slammed it shut, scrambled into the driver's side, put the key in the ignition and locked the door. Only then did she feel safe. Breathing heavily in and out through her nose, she shut her eyes and rested her head on the steering wheel for a good ten to fifteen minutes, trying to regain control of her faculties, trying to slow the rampant beating of her heart.

When she reopened them, it was to two things: a bulky shadow retreating into the back of the parking lot, and an acid-yellow post-it note stuck to the windscreen of her car.

CALL ME, it said, in the messy, childish handwriting of Uriah. Beneath, was his phone number.

She drove out of the parking lot so fast she nearly broke the automatic barrier in two.

———

It is immediately obvious to her what kind of waiting room this is. It's obvious, because it is an exact replica of one she has already visited. It's a woman's health clinic, with a particular role to serve: that of helping women in trouble. Women like Justine.

The waiting room walls are a pale green in colour, green like the grass she'd been lying in only moments before. Space and time move differently here, and she has learned to stop questioning how she can shift from one place to the next so quickly.

Justine is sitting in a chair, the only occupant in the waiting room. She is adrift in a sea of deliberate green. The walls are green, the carpet is green, the rows of plastic chairs are green. There is a water cooler in the corner of the room. Next to that, a cork pinboard with flyers neatly tacked to it with images of smiling, relieved women. Next to that, a clear Perspex magazine rack, from which more smiling women look down upon her. Some of them are folded in half, but half a face still has the power to communicate a message, and that message is simple: *keep smiling,* the half-women say. *No matter what happens, it's important to keep smiling. It'll all be done with soon, and then you can move on with your life, can't you?*

Justine feels sick, and exhausted. At first she assumes the tiredness is from her long climb up the chain-ladder, but it dawns on her as she picks up a pamphlet someone has left lying on the chair to her left, that the tiredness runs deeper than that. That the sickness comes from another part of her aside from trauma. Her senses feel different, too, her nose in particular smelling things with a much greater intensity than she'd ever smelt before. A confusing miasma of scent wafts around her, and her vision swims momentarily as she fights down a rising wave of nausea from the sensory assault. The pamphlet slowly comes back into focus. It is for a rape victim support group. There is a simple outline sketch of two hands holding on the front. *We're here,* it says, beneath the hands. She drops it as if it burns.

A door opposite her opens. Something vast, and monstrous fills the doorway with a hideous silhouette, and then pours itself into the waiting room.

It has a human torso and head, but the body of a slug. Human arms are arranged along its slimy flanks, bent at the elbows, the hands dragging the bulk of its body across the floor towards her. It is clutching a clipboard in one of its skinny, pale hands. The head is female and wearing a smile that is identical to the smiles of the women in the magazine rack. It is a smile that means business.

Justine is more afraid of this smile than anything else she has seen yet in this hell she dug down into.

'Justine?' The thing says, its voice a complex mix of gravelly undertones and sibilant, soft crooning sounds.

She does not answer.

The thing moves closer, its multitude of hands scrabbling for purchase on the green carpet.

'Justine?' It repeats, looking at the clipboard with a frown on its face. 'Are you ready, Justine?'

'Ready for what?' Justine croaks in reply, but she knows. This is another memory, one warped by her surroundings, but a memory nonetheless. In real life, the woman had only had two arms, two legs and the right kind of body for a human, but her smile had been the same. Businesslike. This was a job, to her. She'd seen hundreds of women in her predicament. She was not here to judge. She was here to get the job done. In real life, Justine's Mother had been sitting on the chair to her left, clutching the pamphlet with the holding-hands on the front. Her Mother, who had been a rock throughout everything.

Her poor Mother.

The thing slithers across the floor towards her, still brandishing its clipboard, and she recoils. It puts a hand out, and rests it on her belly. Cold floods her entire body from that one touch, as if all her blood has been replaced with ice.

'You have a baby inside you,' it hisses, and Justine begins to scream. Justine wrenches the clipboard from its grip and hits the nurse-worm full in the face with it. Using the split second this affords her, she leaps from her chair, pushes past, and runs.

'Come back!' the nurse screeches from behind her, using words Justine has heard before.

'There is a baby inside you! You must let us help you!'

Justine finds a door, and slams into it with the full force of her body. The door opens, and...

———

Justine opens a door and finds herself at another party. Not the type of party she used to attend, before Uriah set his sights on her. Not a dinner party with soft jazz music and nice wine and home cooked food and candles. No, this one is the type of party you go to to debase yourself. It's the type of party that pushes a person to their physical limits, the type where anything and everything is on offer

Justine's redundancy hadn't been the restorative opportunity she'd imagined. Instead, she'd found herself on her own, with no financial security and with absolutely no direction or confidence to speak of. She'd given everything to that job, and it still hadn't been enough: she was out on her ass, and the in-jokes, routines, perks, highs and lows of her former place of employment were now all denied to her. It was a bitter pill to swallow, and she did not cope well in the aftermath of her redundancy. But, in a city like hers, private distress was easy to distract yourself from, and there was always a party to go to in order to do so.

And so Justine is here, looking around with a mixture of shock and excitement. She is not sure *why* she is here, only what she hopes to get out of the night: oblivion. A glass tumbler with what looks like expensive whisky in it is handed to her. 'Just another one, then,' she says, and the party notches up a gear. Someone empties a small baggie full of white powder onto a square makeup mirror, a credit card is found, and someone else with a creative bent snips a plastic straw into short, manageable pieces. It does not take long for Justine to gravitate towards the powder like a moth to a flame, and soon she is head-down over the mirror, the straw in her right nostril, the powder burning the back of her throat and working its magic on her gums. For a second, she catches sight of her own reflection in the mirrored surface, and her face is only bone, and little, white maggots wriggle around inside her eye sockets, and behind her, she is sure she can see monstrous things, but then she blinks, and the coke starts to work its magic.

Then, with numb teeth and a growing desire to chew her bottom lip, she pours herself another glass of amber and begins to look around for someone to take home, before the buzz wears off. She does not have a strict criteria: the sex must be emotionless, commitment-free, and end when she wants it to, that is all. Music pounds incessantly, and in the hallway she can see two people already going at it, knickers around slender ankles, parts of themselves on display for everyone to see, and she thinks, suddenly, how silly this all is, what humans do to themselves. The limitations of what we all boil down to, in the end, despite our lofty desires. Eat, shit, fornicate. Die.

But this realisation does not stop her from securing the short-term comfort she craves, and she leaves the party with a tall man lazily wrapped around her in expectation.

Justine has not thought about Uriah once since she left her job, assuming her dealings with him were done the day she threw her crate of belongings into the trunk of her car and put pedal to the floor. The relief of being away from him has been more profound than she'd appreciated, however, because as she makes it outside the party house, one-night-stand in tow, she glances across the street, and freezes in her tracks.

Uriah is standing rigidly on the opposite side of the street, staring at her.

Uriah, with his huge belly, and his angry, red face.

His eyes burn with jealousy, and something else she doesn't understand.

Justine stares at him, incredulous, and then, buoyed by the coke, she shouts at him, another decision she regrets, later.

'Go away, you sad fuck!' she yells, and then, afraid, unsure suddenly, and conscious of her coke bump wearing thin, she turns away and hurries on, head down, back towards her place with her new friend giggling like a teenager in her wake.

'Who the fuck was that guy, your stalker?' he says, with no idea of the seriousness of the situation.

'No-one,' she says curtly, walking faster.

She doesn't look, but she can feel Uriah watching her from down the street.

———

The artificial green of the clinic waiting room fades into a dense, dark green of a forest. Cypress trees, or pines, she doesn't know which, stretch high above her, the bark on the tree trunks thick and scaly like that of an ancient, sun-baked lizard. Thin, sharp blades of grass brush against her ankles, leaving thin, red scratches on her skin.

Justine runs, darting through the trees, tripping over roots and weeds and vines, running from the smiling worm in the clinic, and her clipboard, and the pamphlet, and the folded half-smiles of the magazine women. She is losing her sense of purpose, she realises, as blind panic fades into a general awareness of being lost and alone.

Where is Uriah?

Will she have the strength to do what needs to be done to him, before it's too late? Before her nerve fails completely?

She stops when she reaches a clearing, breath ragged, chest and lungs burning. Before her, she sees a hut. It is old, weathered, with a corrugated iron roof heavily dented by fallen tree branches. Ivy smothers the sides of the hut, and there is a dilapidated veranda out front, peppered with holes and piled high with drifts of pine needles. An old pink couch rots there too, sagging down to the floor. From here it looks like heaped, soft flesh.

Justine feels faint, dizzy. She puts a hand out and leans on a tree for support. Her heart contracts in her chest and she feels as if she is folding inwards, crumpling.

She knows this hut.

She knows this hut very, very well.

And she knows that Uriah will be inside, because, well. This is hell, after all.

And hell is cruel.

Uriah broke into Justine's house while she was fucking the random guy from the party. She had just enough time to realise someone else was in her bedroom, breathing heavily behind her, before she was hit hard across the head with something very heavy. The blow nearly, but not quite, knocked her out. Uriah dragged her onto the floor. Before she sank into the black, she saw Uriah raise his arms up, high over his head. He held a shovel in his hands. He brought it down upon the prone, stunned man in the bed, and Justine fainted.

When she awoke, it was to the hut.

Justine approaches, very, very slowly, one foot in front of the other, which is what people said to her not long after her escape, after Uriah is caught. *One foot in front of the other, dear,* they said, and it was meant kindly, but sometimes she can barely remember where her own feet are or how to operate them, never mind moving them in any sort of coordinated rhythm. The hut fills her vision, and there is a ball of something tight and hot stuck in her throat. Deep down, she's known for a long time that she would have to come back here. She survived, but she has never really left the hut. Never really healed from her time there. The trial was supposed to be part of the healing. Standing before Uriah in court, and letting him see her, alive, uncowed. She had written a victim statement, memorized it, rehearsed it hundreds of times in her bathroom mirror. It was not to be. Uriah had cheated her.

Her anger surges, and she reminds herself of why she is here. She reminds herself of how far she has come. She reminds herself of a promise: not to cower under the shade of the bad things that happened to her. Not to become the poison tree.

Her foot touches down on dry, rotting wood: the verandah steps. It creaks, announcing her presence. She listens for a sign of Uriah. She hears nothing. The forest around her is deathly quiet. No insects, no birds, not even the sound of wind in the trees.

Can she do this, really?

Can she go in there, back to the place where she lost everything?

She mounts the stairs. Sees a door. Her hand hesitates upon the doorknob. She snatches it back, then reaches out again. Yes, yes she can go in there. Because Uriah is in there. Because she has come this far, too far to turn back.

She twists the doorknob.

The door creaks open, and swings smoothly inwards.

———

The inside of the hut is bare, and cold. There is no furniture except for a brand-new mattress on the dirty, old floor. The mattress is covered in a clean white sheet. The contrast is jarring, unexpected. It hurts, but not as much as the memories do.

Justine remembers waking up on that mattress, bound, cold, and in pain from her head wound. She realises, in retrospect, that this new mattress was Uriah's warped attempt at making her feel comfortable. She realises, in retrospect, that Uriah was probably in love with her, in his own, terrible way.

Retrospect and hindsight are terrible things, in Justine's mind. They are clubs with which to beat oneself when the world turns to black.

Justine expected to find Uriah in this hut, waiting for her. She has prepared herself for a fight, for a confrontation, for a desperate showdown, but instead, because hell is cruel, she finds only a small, sad and dishevelled boy, sitting on the mattress with his head in his hands.

In his hand, he has a piece of chalk, and he is using this to scratch something onto the wooden floor of the hut, over and over, as if he has been naughty in school and is being made to write out lines. Justine cannot help it. She watches as he writes, and lets the words sink in as she reads.

Not my fault, they say.

Not my fault.

The boy looks up, sees her standing there. He smiles, unsure, because hell is cruel. Although he is young, a child, Justine can see enough of his features to recognise him.

It is Uriah.

Because hell is cruel.

———

Justine blinks, and sees, for a split second, the man the boy will become. Instead of the child on the mattress, it is Justine, and towering over her, Uriah: triumphant, in control, lost in his own game.

Justine realises that remembering what happens here, reliving it blow by terrible blow, is not why she has come.

She has come to remember what followed. She has come to remind herself that she was stronger than him, in the end, smarter. Because Justine escaped Uriah, eventually. She escaped the hut, despite her own expectation that she would die there alone. He had made a mistake, after planning and rehearsing and following her for so long: he cut through the zip ties that bound her feet and wrists so that he could better arrange her to match the elaborate fantasy he had constructed in his mind. After, a long time after, Justine then got the luckiest break of her entire life. A tiny, tiny window of opportunity as Uriah turned his back to her and sat on the floor to feed his tired legs into his discarded jeans. She took it. She bolted, ran naked through the woods, ran faster than she thought humanly possible, kept running, until she hit a road, and flagged down a passing car.

Hours later, Uriah handed himself into the local police, and confessed everything. Because Uriah was clever like that. Uriah was thinking of the end game: the trial. Being in the hut, Justine came to realise, then, was only the beginning. What came after was, in lots of ways, worse.

Justine wipes away angry tears and the man is a boy once more.

'I did you a favour, you know,' says the boy, using words that are too old for his young mouth.

Justine stares, trying to understand his thought process.

'A favour?'

'Extenuating circumstances.' The boy keeps writing *Not my fault* on the floor, making columns and houses and towers out of his words: a landscape of blame avoidance.

'Extenuating...what?'

'Extenuating circumstances.' The boy pronounces the words slowly, as if it is Justine who is the child.

He continues, head bent in concentration as he writes.

'Things in my past, things that made me what I am today. That's what they will talk about, in court. How it's not my fault, not really. My behaviour is all a product of my childhood. They'll get testimonials from people I used to know, backing it up. My lawyer is good with words like that.' The boy points to the words on the wooden floor and grins.

Not my fault.

Justine feels sick. Uriah was always clever, so much more clever than she gave him credit for.

'I don't care,' she says. 'You owe me. I had a right to face you. A trial.'

The boy shakes his head. 'Not my fault,' he says, and carries on scratching words in chalk upon the floor.

Justine balls her fists up in anger.

Boy Uriah shakes his head, continues. 'It's not like I'll go away for a long time, anyway,' he says, and there is something sad about the way he avoids her eyes. 'Besides, jail doesn't scare me. That's not why I did it.'

'Did...what?' Justine is lost, so terribly, confusedly lost, trying to keep up with his terrifying logic.

'Hung myself. Did you forget? I'm dead like you are now. I didn't do it because I felt bad or frightened of the trial.'

'You did it to fuck with me,' says Justine through gritted teeth.

'I did it because I knew I couldn't have you again. Not completely. You broke my heart, Justine.'

Justine cannot hear this anymore, cannot bear her suffering to be so corrupted. She does none of the things she planned on doing by coming here, by digging down into hell and finding Uriah. She realises, instead that she has made a terrible, terrible mistake. That putting one foot in front of the other means doesn't mean marching down into hell to exact revenge or retribution. It means moving forward, slowly, tiny step by tiny step, away from the past, until it hurts a little less, and a little less, and a little less. One foot after the other, out of the dark, and towards the muted light of dawn on the horizon.

She ran from the hut once. She can do it again.

Behind her, she can hear the boy, Uriah, scratching words into the floor, filling the space there with lies.

She runs.

But it is night-time, now, outside the hut. She runs anyway. She runs right into a tree, head connecting hard with the trunk, and then she cannot hear the boy with his chalk, cannot hear anything, because, despite aiming for a lost light on a lost horizon, she is back in the dark, and the dark is complete.

———

Justine wakes.

She is standing in her house, gripping her phone with white, trembling hands. A voice is speaking to her from her cell. She blinks, trying to place it.

Then she realises.

It is Michael, her lawyer.

'Yeah,' he says, in an off-handedly concerned sort of way. 'I just wanted to check that you are okay, you know. Before tomorrow.'

'Tomorrow?' She croaks, tears forming in her eyes. She can hear her Mother bustling about, washing dishes in the kitchen.

Home.

She is home.

'The trial? Justine, are you okay? I need you to be as focussed as you can. We don't want to give the defence anything to hang off of, do you understand? The Jury will be on your side, don't worry. But we need to keep it together, just a little longer. You just have to get through tomorrow, and then it's over. Okay?'

Justine asks a question, her pulse racing.

'Uriah...is going to stand trial?'

Michael tries, and fails, to hide his concern. 'Yes, Justine, what's going on? Are you okay?'

'Uriah...is not dead?'

Michael snorts. 'What are you talking about? Have you...are you taking your meds, Justine?'

Justine begins to smile.

She has done it.

She went to hell, and she brought him back. Just like she said she would. Tears course freely down her face.

'Justine?' Michael was becoming exasperated.

'I'm fine,' she managed, eventually. 'Just...it's a big day tomorrow, like you said.'

'Did you rehearse your victim statement?' he asked, but Justine has heard enough. She hangs up on him and moves across to the window. She looks out.

And sees herself sleeping.

Justine wakes.

She is in a hospital bed. Her mother is asleep in a chair beside her, head resting on the bed next to her left hand. She raises it cautiously, examining the skin there. Bandages wrap themselves around her wrist. She lifts her other hand: there is a matching bandage there too.

A television plays on silent in the corner of the room. The news is on. A picture of Uriah fills the screen. Underneath, a strip of moving text which says, in capitals:

Local man commits suicide one day before he is due to stand trial....Local man commits....

Over and over, like chalk words on the floor. Saying something ten times in a row doesn't make it any easier to swallow as a truth.

But Justine realises something as she lies there, adjusting to the fact that she is not dead, adjusting to the fact that she is not in hell, adjusting to the truth that Uriah is still dead and will now, forevermore, always be dead and beyond her reach.

Justine realises, slowly, curiously, that she might have something in her heart other than rage, and fear, and disappointment. She realises that what she is, right now, bandaged and bruised and lying in this hospital bed, is a layer of her, a single, burned, ruined layer that can, in time, be peeled away, to reveal different, white, unblemished flesh, and new life, and fresh purpose, away from revenge.

Outside, the night sky is dropping down, studded with stars. Justine looks at them through the blinds on the window and pushes her hands into her pockets as she does so, her mind reeling with emotion. She feels something hard, small and cold brush against the fingertips of her right hand.

She brings it out, looks down at it. Her vision is blurred with tears, but eventually, she makes it out.

It is a small thing, a simple thing, with great value attached to it.

It is a coin.

The Ferryman has returned her fare.

AUTHOR BIO

Gemma Amor is a Bram Stoker Award nominated horror fiction author, podcaster and voice actor based in the UK. Her books include *Cruel Works of Nature*, *Dear Laura*, *White Pines*, *Girl on Fire*, *Six Rooms*, *Grief is a False God*, and *These Wounds We Make*. Her debut traditionally published novel *Full Immersion* is out now from Angry Robot Books

Justine was originally published in Amor's collection, These Wounds We Make.

Afterword

Thank you for picking up this issue of ***Tales From Between***. We hope you enjoyed it. If you would like to support us (and never miss a thing we publish) please consider joining us over on Patreon: patreon.com/TalesFromBetween

FOLLOW US ON TWITTER:
@from_between

JOIN OUR MAILING LIST:
talesfrombetween.wordpress.com/contact

TALES
FROM
BETWEEN